THE DEVIL'S DOLLAR SIGN

The Man With No Name stood six feet four inches tall ... He wore a poncho that fell to his knees in the front and the back ... He smoked Mexican cigarros and hunted for men for the money on their heads.

The Reverend had a face chiseled like that of an Indian ... It was dark as sin, with sharp cheekbones and a pointed chin ... He wore a long frock-coat and carried an oversized Bible that hid a sharp-shooting gun.

They clashed because of the gold. And now one of them would have to die ...

Other 'Dollar' Westerns

THE DEVIL'S DOLLAR SIGN

Joe Millard

A STAR BOOK

published by
the Paperback Division of
W. H. ALLEN & Co. Ltd

A Star Book
First published in Great Britain by
Universal Tandem Publishing Co. Ltd 1973
Reprinted 1977 by
Tandem Publishing Ltd
This edition reprinted 1980, 1984 by
The Paperback Division of
W. H. Allen & Co. Ltd
A Howard and Wyndham Company
44 Hill Street, London W1X 8LB

First published in the United States by
Universal Publishing and Distributing Corporation 1972

Cover photograph by permission of United Artists

Printed in Great Britain by
Hunt Barnard Printing Ltd, Aylesbury, Bucks.

ISBN 0 352 30743 9

Prologue

Shortly after the Louisiana Purchase in 1803, President Jefferson dispatched several teams of investigators to learn what exactly the United States had acquired. Of these, the most famous, the Lewis and Clark expedition to the Pacific, overshadowed all the others. But others were contributing mightily to a knowledge of the Southwest.

One of these, a team of cartographers, was sent to survey and map a vast section which was in the process of being erected as a U.S. Territory. In time they came upon a canyon, magnificent, somber, brooding, yet blood-tingling in excitement. They measured, studied, surveyed and reported it with the romantic name, supposedly Indian, of Chi-ra-oo-na Canyon. Someone with magnificent effrontery translated this as "Grand" or "awe-inspiring," which seemed to fit, although none of the team had the slightest knowledge of the Indian tongue.

Perhaps two decades later, new and more cynical arrivals in the area had already discovered the Indians' talent for earthy, dead-pan humor, particularly at the expense of the invading palefaces. With tongue firmly in cheek, they hoped that none of the cartographers had stepped in a fresh mound of *Chi-ro-oo-na*, left by a buffalo that had been feeding upon what the pioneers realistically named "Loose-End Weed."

However, the point is that the cartographic reports filed in 1804 and 1805 (still available somewhere in the Smithsonian or War Department archives, I am sure) made no mention of the Devil's Dollar Sign. Either it was not there at the time of their exploration, or they overlooked it. The latter suggestion is unthinkable, since they were in the canyon at the time of year when the position of the sun made the immense carving stand out in harsh clarity against the dull, drab rock of the cliff's face.

Hence we may pretty much accept the fact that the sign

5

was *not* on the cliff in 1804–05, but definitely *was* there some four decades later when early settlers and passers-through renamed the colossal chasm "Dollar Sign Canyon." Out of these roots was to grow a staggering mystery.

No one could possibly deny that the sign was an unmistakable U.S. dollar sign, though with a minor difference. It was deeply carved into the sandstone face of the cliff some five hundred feet up from the canyon floor. No one had ever bothered to measure, while it was still in existence, but eyewitnesses generally agreed that the capital "S" was a good hundred feet in height from lower to upper curves. Whatever its origin, it had to have been a stupendous undertaking.

The difference (and this was what, quite literally, drove some men mad) was in the single vertical line that converted the "S" into a true dollar sign. It was in the form of an arrow with the arrowhead pointing downward. More mystifying, it was not precisely vertical but had a barely noticeable slant from upper right to lower left.

Clearly, the slant was deliberately done. But for what purpose? The first and most obvious conclusion was that the arrow pointed to some form of fabulous riches—a lost mine, perhaps, or hidden Spanish treasure looted from the empire of the Aztecs.

Men killed one another or themselves or drove themselves mad with frustration in their frenzied, futile search for the secret. The spot on the canyon floor where the arrow seemed to point was pitted with holes dug in a vain search for buried wealth.

Most maddening of all, below the arrow's point and in direct line with it were several dark spots that might be only shadows, or they might be caves. There seemed no possible way to reach them to find out. A number of men had fallen to their deaths trying to climb the crumbling face of the sheer sandstone cliff.

To be let down from the top by rope was equally impossible. That part of the cliff bearing the dollar sign was an immense, jutting overhang. Anyone getting past this by a rope would find himself dangling in midair, a full hundred feet out from the face of the cliff.

Shortly after the middle of the century, the frantic search came to an abrupt and bloody end. Until then, the Indians of the region had held the dollar sign in superstitious awe, convinced that the carving was the handiwork of a dark and evil spirit. No red man could be persuaded or coerced into setting foot inside Dollar Sign Canyon. During this period the white treasure seekers had free rein, with no fear of attack by marauding Indians as long as they were in the canyon.

Then a large band of particularly bloodthirsty and restless young braves, loosely related to the Chiricahuas (the pioneers called them Cherry Cows) quarreled with the rest of the tribe and broke away. Under a savage leader named Pa-Ha-Eta, or Bloody Hand, they launched a campaign of terror, torture, plunder and murder that virtually paralyzed the lower end of the Territory.

The braves were rebels in every sense and one of the things against which they rebelled was the traditional fear of Dollar Sign Canyon. With consummate eloquence Bloody Hand persuaded his followers that the somber canyon would be a perfect refuge and headquarters. Why fear the dark spirit of evil, he argued, when they themselves were evil personified? And what better symbol of their plunderings than the white man's sign of riches?

There were a dozen treasure seekers in the canyon when the band moved in. All were killed and scalped. The more fortunate ones died quickly.

Astonishingly, one white man who had lived in the canyon since before modern memory, was not only spared but permitted to continue occupying his cave at the base of the cliff. He was a great, wasted giant of a man, stooped as if from the burden of carrying an immense tangle of dirty white hair and beard. He wore a flowing robe that had once been white and shuffled along, bent over and leaning on a shepherd's crook. On one foot he wore a thonged sandal and on the other, an Indian moccasin, badly scuffed and missing a large part of its decorative beading.

The only name by which he was known was Herkimer the Mad Hermit. The title fit, for mad he unquestionably was in the fullest sense. Yet it was this madness that had bought him immunity over the years from torture and death at the hands of the Indians.

To most tribes, an insane person was held in superstitious awe as having been personally set apart from other men by the Great Spirit. So Bloody Hand, having defied other superstitions, bowed to this one and spared old Herkimer's life. Not only was the hermit permitted to go on occupying his barren cave but from time to time, after a successful raid on some rancher's herd, they shared their meat with the old man.

In his more lucid moments, Herkimer claimed to be a hundred and nineteen years old. He swore that as a boy he had personally witnessed the carving of the dollar sign on the cliff. He insisted that he alone knew not only *who* had carved it, but *why*, and what the symbol's hidden message actually was. But, since most of his mouthings were a meaningless babble, very few persons paid more than passing attention to his claims.

In time, some of those who ignored them were destined to be very sorry that they had not listened more carefully to the old hermit's vaporings.

Chapter 1

Some men seemed destined to go through life, or what little is granted them, dogged by persistent misfortune. Nothing they attempt ever turns out as it should. Their zigzag path is strewn with calamities, not of their direct making. They seem to be the helpless victims of a capricious and ill-intentioned fate no matter what they do.

It was with good reason that the outlaw, Samson Beals, was listed on the reward posters tacked to the walls of sheriffs' offices across the Southern Territory as "Bad-Luck Beals." It was also the reason the bounty posted on his head, dead or alive, was a paltry one thousand dollars. He was far more guilty of intent than of execution. Most of his earnest efforts at crime had turned into grotesque and often bloody fiascos.

This time, he vowed, was going to be different. Every step had been planned meticulously to the last detail. Every conceivable thing that could go wrong had been anticipated and prepared for. Although an accident had tipped him off to the opportunity in the first place, there was no allowance for further accidents on Bad-Luck's careful program. From that point on, everything would go like clockwork.

The accident that started the wheels turning was the unexpected meeting of two men with a deep secret and an old pal with a convivial urge to buy drinks.

In Shakespeare's immortal *Merchant of Venice*, the Bard remarks that "there are some who, when the bagpipe sings i' the nose, cannot contain their urine. . . ." This might be aptly paraphrased as "there are some who, when John Barleycorn sings i' the glass, cannot contain their secrets."

Bad-Luck was drowning his sorrows in a saloon ironically named *The Lucky Shot* on the day it happened. Two men next to him at the bar were quietly drinking and

9

conversing in earnest whispers. The few fragments of conversation that reached his ears were too innocuous to stir any interest.

The man nearest him banged down his empty glass and said, "That's my limit, Alf. One more and I'd either start singing or talkin' my damfool head off."

"Me, too, Sam," his companion agreed. "If you're smart enough to know when enough's enough, I'll go along with you."

They were turning away from the bar when the batwing doors flapped open and a big man barged in. He stopped short, a smile of happy recognition lighting his face.

"I'll be a dirty apple-picker," he boomed. "Sam Ellison, of all people. I haven't seen you since the Spondulix closed."

He rushed across and there was a great pumping of hands and slapping of backs and an effusion of "well, wells," and "goddams!" Alf was duly introduced to one Thorny Somebody-or-other, "my old bunk mate in Spondulix."

"By God!" Thorny said again, wagging his head. "Three years since I seen you last. This calls for a celebration and I got the poke to bankroll it. Barkeep, the drinks are on me."

"Now I don't know," Sam said, scowling. "I just kind of figgered I'd had enough and Alf, here, went along with me on it. On account of we've got jobs now, we can't get fallin'-down stoned at this time of day."

"Sam-u-el," Thorny roared. "Three years, boy. Three goddam years since we was the best of friends an' drinkin' companions. Do you mean to stand there with your bare face hangin' to hell out and tell me you're too goddam hoity-toity to have a drink with your old chum? You mean you've forgot what we done to that whorehouse in Pima Flats?" He leaned around to point a cocked finger at Alf. "Now *you* strike me as the kind of fella ain't too good to drink with a friend. How about it?"

"Well," Alf said weakly, "mebbe just one."

"Awright, awright," Sam said. "Just one, ol' friend."

At the first mention of Spondulix Bad-Luck had stiffened, every sense suddenly alert. The three were on his right, which was not too good. Bad-Luck's right ear had never been too good since a gunfight in which a companion had loosed two forty-five blasts just off his right shoulder.

He signaled for a refill of his glass, then with elaborate indifference turned around with his back to the bar, hooking his elbows over the rim and nursing his drink. This put his sound left ear toward the trio and the electrifying key word—Spondulix—the slang term for riches.

It was also the name of one of the most fabulous mines in the Territory, as well as the mining settlement that had grown up around it. The very name "Spondulix" was the trade name for prosperity. If you had enough Spondulix you were rich and if you had a piece of the Spondulix Mine, you had it in spades. In its brief heyday it rivaled any treasure trove in the West. But overnight the fabulous vein had petered out, the mine was abandoned, the settlement of the same name turned into a ghost town.

Yet there were the die-hards and the know-alls who insisted that the failure of one vein meant nothing. Where there was one horde, they insisted, there had to be more, and the ownership was too slack in blithely writing off the whole property of one of the world's great mines on little more than a whim. Now there were wild and baseless rumors circulating that a new and even richer vein had been found and that the Spondulix was about to spring to life once more.

The one drink turned into two and three and even four. At this point, Thorny leaned close and bellowed in a stentorian whisper, "Level with me, Sam. In them days you was their top guard at the mine. Is there any truth in them rumors that they've discovered a new vein of ore that's richer'n any before?"

Sam blinked bloodshot eyes and peered around in an alcoholically-exaggerated pantomine of security. Alf looked worried.

"Don't breathe it to a soul," Sam husked in a whisper that rattled windows a block away, "but you're absolutely right. The new vein is ten times richer than the one that started them off. The Spondulix is producing ore like never before, but they're keepin' it quiet. Seems they's a couple of the original owners are real bastards they wanna push out. They figger as long as they don't know it's payin' off again, they can be pressured into sellin' out for peanuts. So they ain't lettin' out that the mine is payin' off like Croesus on a drunk. Nobody's supposed to know until they've bought out the bastards for pennies."

Sam swayed on his feet, staring at his friend through red-veined eyes. He laid a finger to his lips and loosed a *shushhh!* that would have shamed a steam calliope.

"You know you can trust me," Thorny whispered, *sotto voce,* "I wouldn't tell my own mother what you've jes' tol' me, ol' chum. So the Spondulix is pourin' it out again. By God, I know one or two who'd be goddam happy to hear about that. But, of course, I wouldn't say it to *anybody.*"

Sam slapped his friend on the back. "I knew I could trust you, ol' frien', ol' bygod frien', you old sonomabitsh, you."

Alf tugged at his sleeve and said worriedly, "Sam, you think maybe we said enough?"

"Not half enough," Sam bawled. "By God, it's time the rest of the world knowed how we keep our secrets." He appealed to the rest of the bar crowd. "How 'bout that, huh? Do you all know the secrets we keep, huh?"

Bad-Luck slapped down a silver dollar, eased himself out from the bar and scurried away. His first stop was the office of mine registry. When he departed he had a complete list of all owners of the Spondulix Mine. There were five names on the registry books. Three of them were veteran investors, experienced in the vagaries of their profession, particularly in the ups and downs of mining development. If anyone was being brutally squeezed out, it would be the two unknowns, well-heeled babes-in-the-woods, who had already reaped a profit but who were being frozen out of a far greater return.

Both unknowns were in Texas, but a brief session in an alley with a cattle buyer who believed in fairy tales provided the eating and traveling money needed. Bad-Luck was jubilant when he emerged from the two meetings. He even gave serious consideration to distributing a notice to sheriffs' and marshals' offices that henceforth he was to be known as Good-Luck Beals. If unannounced visits to the Spondulix Mine confirmed his assertion that mining operations had been secretly resumed, he would be assured of thirty-five hundred dollars in reward money, guaranteed by legally processed agreements.

This, however, was only modest but welcome side money. A few days spent reconnoitering the mine by telescope from a distant mesa not only confirmed its reopening but supplied him with even more vital information.

Promptly every Wednesday the week's accumulation of rich findings was padlocked into a gray Wells Fargo box and carried by freight wagon, guarded by four heavily armed and determined men, to a junction point with the regular Wells Fargo stage route. Here it was put aboard a W-F stagecoach for the run to El Paso. The transfer was made quickly, quietly and without fanfare. The time of transfer was an unvarying three o'clock in the afternoon.

Despite his consistent run of foul luck, Bad-Luck Beals was not without imagination. On Tuesday the sheriff received an official-looking invitation to appear with his most trusted deputies at a lawmen's meeting in Albuquerque. It was suggested that, since Wednesday was an off day for major crimes, his minor deputy could take over the office for a few hours. The sheriff, newly elected and highly flattered, accepted at once and made immediate arrangements to leave the office in full charge of Assistant Deputy Merrill Adams, a move that postponed Adams's firing for a week or ten days.

As his final move, Bad-Luck arranged through a talented acquaintance who owed him money that a broken axle would delay the Wells Fargo passenger run over the same route for another hour. Every possible contingency had thus been anticipated and arranged for.

Every contingency, in fact, except that Wednesday happened to be the day that an outlaw chieftain named Monteregno had chosen to stick up the local bank. It turned out to be a day of great good fortune for Monteregno and great bad fortune for Bad-Luck Beals. But that's how the dice fall, sometimes. Or, for the Bad-Luck Bealses of this world, most of the time.

Wednesday afternoon found Bad-Luck at a sharp curve in the stagecoach road, engaged in an endeavor he despised—physical labor. In this case it was the labor of chopping down a tree so that it would fall across and block the stage. Meanwhile, a couple of miles up that road, the week's rich findings from the Spondulix Mine were being loaded into the boot of the Wells Fargo coach.

The tree crashed down exactly where it was supposed to, which was an omen to Bad-Luck Beals. So few things in his messed-up life had done what they were supposed to do at the right time. Almost immediately he heard the crash and clatter of the approaching stagecoach. He had cut it fine, but not quite too fine. For once his timing was impeccable.

He swung into the saddle of his waiting horse, pulled up the bandanna handkerchief that masked his face and hauled his rifle from its boot. The coach rattled around the curve and was hauled up with a great roaring and cursing by the driver and a chorus of indignant shouts from passengers who had found themselves unceremoniously on the floor.

Beside the driver, the shotgun guard had his weapon to his shoulder and was glaring around, knowing from harsh experience the import of the newly felled tree. Bad-Luck took careful aim and shot the guard through the head. The guard pitched off the coach seat, carrying his shotgun with him. Bad-Luck felt a new surge of confidence at this added proof that today was indeed to be his day to change his nickname.

The driver was hauling on the reins of his four-horse team, bawling, "Don't shoot me, fer gawd's sake! I ain't armed."

"I won't," Bad-Luck said, riding out from among the trees, "providin' you do what you're told and don't try no monkeyshines. Climb down and unload the boot. Dump ever'thing right there in the road, and make damn sure the Spondulix box is with it."

"Yes, *sir*, sir," the driver said eagerly, scrambling down. "Th-that'll be the first out, sir."

There were two gray Wells Fargo boxes plus the passengers' luggage, including a pair of matched cases that looked expensive enough to yield unguessable riches. Bad-Luck licked his lips behind the bandanna and gestured with his rifle.

"Get back up and get movin'. You can work around the top of the tree if you're careful—and you *better* be careful."

"Yes, *sir*," the driver said, clambering back to his seat.

He was gathering up the reins and easing off the brake when there was a thunder of hoofbeats and a dozen heavily armed men came pounding around the bend in the trail. Bad-Luck had no way of knowing that this was a posse pursuing Monteregno, whose bank holdup had been an unqualified success. He only saw that this was the time to get elsewhere in one helluva hurry. He got!

He had a small lead because the posse stopped to check the coach and help the shaken driver replace the boxes and luggage in the boot. They felt no great urgency, since the direction of Bad-Luck's flight was into a waterless area of badlands where no one could survive for long.

From long and bitter experience, however, Bad-Luck had learned the region far more intimately than his pursuers. He headed for what, at a distance, appeared to be a solid cliff, but proved to be a deceptive wall of rock a few yards in front of the cliff itself. Surrounding this was a great bed of time-hardened lava from some ancient eruption on which not even a herd of iron-shod elephants could leave a track.

Safely hidden behind the rock shield, Bad-Luck listened as the posse thundered by and bitterly cursed his heritage of misfortune. Nothing in this day's happenings would change or improve his image. He would continue to be Bad-Luck Beals, the ultimate symbol of perpetual frustration.

Behind him a voice said, "*Tch! Tch!* Such language is an affront to thy Maker."

Bad-Luck whirled, his gun fairly leaping from its holster into his hand, and his jaw dropped. A few yards behind him, astride a mule, was a very tall man wearing a long frock coat and clerical collar and clutching a huge family Bible to his chest. His free hand was out in a placating gesture.

"You goddam dummox," Bad-Luck snarled. "Ain't you got no better sense than to sneak up behind a fella wearin' a gun?"

"Peace, brother," the stranger said. "I was not *sneaking*. I merely rode in behind you. If you failed to hear me, I am not to blame. I am the Reverend Leemon Fairfeather."

"Okay, Reverend," Bad-Luck snapped. "Unhitch your gun and let it drop first; then we jabber."

The Reverend Fairfeather smiled sadly and opened the frock coat to show that he wore no gun belt or holstered pistol.

"Oh, ye of little faith. See for yourself that the only weapon I carry is one far more powerful than that gun in your hand. The Word in this book is my shield and my buckler."

"Yeah? You think a forty-five slug wouldn't go through

that like it was only paper? So you're a lousy mush-mouthed psalm-singer, but that don't give you no right to sneak up behind me. I ain't in the market for anything you'd be peddlin', parson, so take your shield and buckles and beat it to hell out of my sight."

"The wicked," the Reverend Fairfeather said gloomily, "shall flourish and then wither, like the green bay tree. But obviously, you can't be as wicked as you pretend, because to judge by your unfortunate nickname of Bad-Luck Beals, you have clearly failed to flourish."

Bad-Luck's face displayed a grotesque blend of rage and suspicion. He thumbed back the hammer of the pistol.

"You smart sonuvabitch! Talk up and talk fast. How come you know who I am? Who are you and what's your game?"

"He who notes even the fall of a sparrow would scarcely fail to know the identity of a ruthless killer of an innocent stagecoach guard. And, as I told you, I am the Reverend Leemon Fairfeather and my game, as you call it, is freeing men from the consequences of their own evil."

"Oh, shut up, shut up, *shut up!*" Bad-Luck yelled. "Talk, talk, talk, fer crissake! You're up to here with a bunch of goddam words that don't mean nothin'. So you go to hell your way and I'll go mine and stay outa my life, you bastard."

He slapped his gun back into its holster, whirled his horse around and started out from behind the rock. The Reverend Fairfeather sighed and opened his huge Bible at a spot marked by a scarlet ribbon. Inside, the blank pages had been hollowed out to form a nest for a custom-made forty-four pistol with an enormous fourteen-inch barrel.

"Repent and abandon your wicked ways," he said and shot Bad-Luck Beals in the back.

As the late Bad-Luck pitched out of his saddle, his dead hands still clutched the reins so that his horse was jerked to an abrupt halt. The Reverend Fairfeather eyed the body sadly, then got out a small notebook. He turned to the second page, labeled "B" and ran a finger down a list of names and figures until he came to one marked: "Bad-Luck Beals—$1,000."

He plucked a forty-four caliber bullet from his pocket and used the lead end as a pencil to cross off the notation, humming softly to himself.

Chapter 2

The sheriff of San Quenada had never seen his visitor before in his life but he recognized him instantly, by rumor and reputation. After all, a man standing six feet four, wearing a Mexican poncho that fell to his knees front and back and smoking a stubby Mexican *cigarro* would be hard-pressed to remain anonymous. This could only be the notorious Man With No Name, the deadly bounty killer.

Try as he would, the sheriff could not keep his weathered face from revealing his opinion of those who made a trade of hunting down their fellow men for profit. The newcomer ignored the expression, having encountered it in varying forms for a greater part of his life. If sheriffs were half as competent at capturing outlaws as they were at capturing votes, his would be a profitless trade at best.

He edged along the side of the room, studying the reward notices tacked to the wall. Most were familiar from having been seen on sheriffs' office walls from one end of the Territory to the other. Some were yellowed with age. He turned abruptly and rapped a knuckle against one of the more recent.

"This Bad-Luck Beals—is the offer still open?"

"Funny you should ask that today of all days," the sheriff said. "Just this morning a preacher feller lugged in Bad-Luck's corpus, shot in the back."

"Preacher?"

"So he said. The Reverend ..." he scrabbled in a drawer of his desk and found a receipt form. "Reverend Leemon Fairfeather. Claimed somebody else shot Bad-Luck and he just happened to stumble on his body, but I ain't so sure I believe him. I've seen warmer, friendlier eyes on a rattlesnake. He made out like he didn't even know about the bounty till he happened to spot Bad-Luck's picture on the poster there."

17

"He took it, though?"

"You damn bet he took it. Said it would help finance his labor in the vineyards, whatever the hell *that* means. If there's any vineyards in this Territory, *I* never heard of 'em. He took it and cleared out so fast he screwed hisself out of a thousand dollars. This mornin' Bad-Luck held up a Wells Fargo stage and shot the guard. Not twenty minutes after this preacher feller leaves, I get a telegram— Wells Fargo and the Spondulix Mine crowd are uppin' the bounty to two thousand."

"Spondulix," the hunter said, his eyebrows climbing. "I thought they closed up when the vein petered out."

"So'd most ever'body, includin' me. But it seems they've hit a new vein that's richer'n the old one. They're operatin' but tryin' to keep it quiet so's they can squeeze out a couple of the fellas that bankrolled 'em to begin with. But if you ask me, there's somethin' mighty fishy about the whole deal. . . ."

"Fishy? In what way?"

"That ain't none of your business, friend. Just forget my mouth run away with my good sense there for a minute."

The hunter shrugged noncommittally. "What sort of a looking gent is this Reverend Fairfeather?"

"Big," the sheriff said. "Big as you, I'd guess. And a face like an Indian's—dark as sin, with stickin'-out cheekbones and narrowin' down to a pointy chin. Put a handle on it and you could use it to chop trees. Wears a long frock coat and carries the biggest goldang Bible I ever did see. But cold eyes. One look and they'd freeze the balls off a brass monkey."

"Much obliged for your time, sheriff," the hunter said. "I'll be pushing along."

He turned and went out quickly. A moment later the pound of hooves receded down the street. The sheriff scratched his head, scowling.

"Now, what do you suppose is cookin' in that sonuvabitch's mind? He's sure as hell got a bug in his britches about somethin'."

The Reverend Fairfeather hummed contentedly to himself as his mule jogged steadily southward. It had not been a sensational day, but a good day nonetheless. In his pattern of operation, any day that showed a profit, however modest, was a success, and a thousand dollars was nothing to sneeze at. Now he was about to launch the most stupendous scheme of his career, one in which the potential for profit was staggering.

The mule slowed to a spine-jolting trot, then to a walk and finally stopped with its nose almost against a sheer cliff. The Reverend Fairfeather hauled the animal's head around sharply and guided it into an almost invisible slit through the rock. The slit became a narrow, winding passage that opened eventually into a small, hidden valley.

In this valley one Eddie "Big Butch" Quant was giving final instructions to his men, as vicious a pack of cut-throats as the Territory could boast.

"Now get this and get it straight, those of you who just joined up. As soon as we pull off the job we split up and everybody comes back here at a different time and by a different route. And make mighty damn sure you ain't followed. All the time we've been usin' this hideout, no-body's ever found it yet and we ain't about to . . . about to . . ." His voice trailed off. His mouth opened and closed but no sound came forth.

Then the shocked paralysis broke. With a strangled yell, he leaped to his feet, grabbing his gun. The others scrambled up, snatching their guns, then froze, gaping incredulously at the sight of the Reverend Leemon Fairfeather, sitting on his mule a few yards away, clutching his enormous Bible.

"Peace, brothers," the Reverend said, pulling the frock coat wide to show his empty waist. "As you see, I wear no gun so you can put away your weapons. I put my trust in the Good Book and it has never yet failed me in time of need."

"A parson, for God's sake!" Big Butch exploded. "How in hell did you ever find your way in here?"

The Reverend Fairfeather smiled benignly. "My steps are directed by an infallible guide, Mr. Quant."

Big Butch loosed a howl of wordless rage.

"How come you know me by name, damn yuh? Who the hell are you and what's your game? Cut out the bull-crap and hand out a little straight talk."

"I'm the Reverend Leemon Fairfeather and my game, as you call it, is showing men like yourselves the road to a better life. As for recognizing you, Mr. Quant, that was not difficult. The artist who drew your portrait was quite competent."

He drew a folded paper from inside the cover of the big Bible and tossed it over. Big Butch, looking dazed, caught the paper and unfolded it. The sheet proved to be a WANTED poster bearing his likeness and the announcement that a five-thousand-dollar bounty would be paid to anyone delivering Big Butch Quant or his dead body to the sheriff of San Quenada.

"Damn your hide!" Butch yelled, the gun shaking violently in his hand. "So that's what you are—a stinkin' bounty hunter. Well, this is one bounty you ain't gonna live long enough to collect."

"Before you kill me," the Reverend Fairfeather said calmly, "I suggest you read *this* poster carefully."

He tossed down a second paper, somewhat larger than the other. This one bore an excellent likeness of the Man With No Name, complete with his poncho, flat black hat and stubby *cigarro*.

A stark black headline screamed: REWARD—$50,000— REWARD! Following this was a detailed description of The Man With No Name which finished, "The reward will be paid for the delivery of said bounty hunter, dead or alive but preferably dead, to any member of the OOA." It was signed, *"Organized Outlaws Association."* Below this, in smaller type, was a long list of names.

Butch and the men crowded around him goggled at the poster, then at the man on the mule, who returned a bland and unruffled smile. The outlaw chieftain suddenly loosed a roar of outrage.

"What the hell? There's *my* name down there on that list. What's this supposed to be—some kinda joke or something?"

"If the bounty hunter thinks it's a joke, he could very well die laughing. But when a few hundred of these reward notices are posted from El Paso to Yuma and every professional and amateur gunslinger in the Southwest sets out to collect the reward, I have a feeling he will find the idea distinctly *unfunny.*"

"I don't get it," Butch said hoarsely. "I don't get it at all. I never *heard* of this Organized Outlaws deal, so how could my name get on here?"

"It's simple, Butch. You never heard of the Organized Outlaws Association for the good reason that it's newly organized and has just moved into this Territory. You are on the list because it was compiled from reward posters and covers men with bounties of three thousand dollars or more on their heads. They have the most to gain by joining, because they are the ones the bounty killer preys on. Each could live a richer, freer life if he is dead. So, to bring that about, each is expected to contribute a share of the reward. You are down to pledge five thousand dollars as your share."

"Why the hell should I?" Butch roared indignantly. "He ain't never bothered none of us and ain't likely to. He never even got this far south from all I heard about him."

"Brace yourself for some bad news, friend Butch," the Reverend Fairfeather said coldly. "The bounty killer is here right now and I'm quite certain he didn't make the trip just to admire the scenery. He has, in fact, spent some time this afternoon closeted with Sheriff Dobrin of San Quenada, studying reward notices."

Big Butch Quant cursed thickly. His men cast nervous looks toward the narrow entrance to their valley. The Reverend watched them with cynical amusement.

"Precisely my point," he murmured.

"By God!" Butch bawled. "If that bastard comes sneakin' ..."

"Spare me your empty bluster," The Reverend Fairfeather interrupted wearily. "If you know anything at all about the man, you know you're babbling nonsense. His is probably the fastest and deadliest gun in the West. In a shoot-out with the bounty killer, you would look like a ham-handed beginner—and a dead one, to boot."

Butch glared at him sullenly and licked his lips.

"Awright, awright. But tell me one thing, an' tell it straight, not with that parson talk that gabbles on and on and never says nothin'. What's a preacher doing mixed up with a deal like this? Where do *you* fit in?"

"Why," the Reverend Fairfeather said softly, "I'm the one who expects to collect the fifty-thousand-dollar bounty."

Chapter 3

Through the violent years of gunning his way to the top of his trade, the bounty hunter had learned never to underestimate his hunches. True, they usually lured him into situations of extreme danger. But he had also learned that danger and profit generally went hand-in-hand, and the greater the danger, the greater the profit.

Sheriff Dobrin of San Quenada had remarked that there was something "fishy" about the secret reopening of the Spondulix Mine. Then, clearly regretting a slip of the tongue, he had refused to elaborate on the subject. Nothing could have been better calculated to stir the hunter's suspicions and sharpen his interest. His strong hunch had led him first to the local newspaper office for some intense browsing through old issues, then west to the Spondulix Mine and the settlement of the same name.

In its heyday, the mine had been one of the richest producers in the West. The shanty settlement of Spondulix, near the mine head, mushroomed to a roaring boom town that boasted it would be the new capital when the Territory became a state. Then, overnight, the rich vein petered out, the mine closed and the boom town became a ghost town.

Judging from appearances, it was still a ghost town, and that in itself was a mystery. To reopen the mine required a large force of miners. Since miners and their families would have to live somewhere, the old town would be the logical place. But, viewing it from the crest of a low ridge, the only occupants of Spondulix appeared to be pack rats.

The sagging, paintless buildings had a look of desolate emptiness, islands of decay in a sea of weeds. Here and there a forlorn section of broken picket fence still stood erect. The shops and saloons on Main Street were closed and shuttered. A hot, vagrant wind chased balls of tumbleweed along the empty streets. In some places, the board sidewalks were half-buried under drifts of sand.

The air of abandonment was so complete that he touched spurs to the flanks of his bay gelding with the intention of bypassing the town and riding to the mine. Then impulse, or hunch again, made him swerve onto the main street. He rode along at a sedate pace, his sharp gaze shuttling from side to side, seeing nothing to contradict the firm impression of dissolution. Then, suddenly, it was there, sharp before his eyes.

He was riding past the old livery stable, its sign fading under the fierce sun, its double doors shut, its yard empty of the wagons and buggies that had thronged it in the days of prosperity, its watering trough bone dry and cracking. Then he saw the dark patch on the ground at one end of the trough, under the shade of the big box.

He reined in and swung off his horse. The trough was dry, sucked of any moisture by the blazing sun. But in the shade beneath, a patch of the sandy soil was still damp. He straightened then and saw the horse droppings off to one side, under a saguaro's bayonet leaves. They were the rich brown of freshness, not dried to a shriveled kernel as they would be under a day of the blazing sun.

He tramped to the double doors and tried them quietly. As he anticipated, they were barred from within. He left the bay ground-haltered and went around the side of the stable to the rear. A second set of double doors, also closed, faced a smaller yard. This one, however, showed the impress of recent hoofmarks. There were more fresh droppings and wisps of new hay caught in the spines of a cactus.

He cat-footed to the double doors and gave one a gentle shove. It swung inward two or three inches, moving soundlessly on well-oiled pin hinges. He leaped aside, half expecting a fusillade of shots. When none came he reached under the poncho for his gun and thumbed back the hammer.

Using his left hand he pushed the door a few inches further and slipped through, closing it softly behind him. He stood with his back to the door, his gun poised, waiting for his eyes to adjust to the semi-darkness of the interior. For the moments this took, he was completely vulnerable and knew it. Still nothing happened.

Squinting through the gloom he could see no human

figures but eleven horses in stalls along one side, munching newly cured hay. Saddles and gear lay outside each stall and bridles were looped over the low dividing partitions. The mingled smells of hay, manure and fresh horse sweat hung heavily on the air.

He slid his gun back into its holster and moved along the stalls, laying his hand on the flanks of three or four horses. The flesh of each was steamy-hot, the hair soaked with sweat. Streaks of white lather outlined the edges of what had been saddle blankets and cinches. Clearly these animals had been ridden and ridden hard within the past half hour or so.

In any well ordered stable they would have been immediately scraped clean of lather and thoroughly rubbed down. Outlaws, however, tended to be notoriously indifferent to the welfare of their horses, even though their own lives or liberty too often depended upon the speed and endurance of their mounts.

The bounty hunter could see nothing further of interest toward the front of the building. He turned to go back toward the rear and froze. A man was crouched near the doors, covering him with a cocked gun. Through the gloom he could make out an ugly knife-scarred face that looked familiar.

In the depths of his cash-register memory a bell jangled and a tab popped up, bearing a name and a figure. *Ike Fease—five hundred dollars.* It was no great shakes as a bounty, perhaps, but five hundred dollars would cover a lot of expenses during a long-drawn-out pursuit. Rack up another potential score for his hunches.

He took a step forward and the crouching figure snarled, "Stand right where you are, mister, and keep your hands out in plain sight. Then start talking fast and straight. Who the hell are you and what are you doing, sneaking around here?"

The hunter lifted a hand, palm out in a conciliatory gesture.

"Take it easy with that gun, friend. It might be loaded. If you're the stableman, you're the gent I was looking for. I'd like my horse fed, watered and curried while I'm up tending to a little business with the manager of the mine."

Fease's hard eyes narrowed sharply.

"What kind of business?"

"Well, now," the hunter said, "if *you're* the manager of

the mine, I'd prefer to discuss it in your office. If you're *not* the manager, then my business with the manager is none of your business, my friend."

A second roughneck stepped from behind a shadowed stall partition, gun in hand.

"We're making it *our* business, mister, as of right now."

The hunter squinted at the new arrival's long, lantern-jawed face and back in his mind his mental cash register went *bing!* again. The pay-tab popped up, this time with the name of *George Muggins* and the sum of *seven hundred fifty dollars*. The ante was climbing most comfortably.

"Awright," Muggins rasped. "What give you the idea there'd be a manager at a mine that petered out and closed down a good three years ago?"

"I get around," the hunter said smugly, "and I hear things."

"Things like what?"

"Oh, like about a new vein, richer than the first, and a chestful of gold dust that's put on board the Wells Fargo coach every Wednesday. Will they do for openers?"

"You hear that, George?" Ike Fease yelped. "This wise guy is too wise—too goddam wise to go on living."

"Now you two listen to me," the hunter broke in, pitching his voice to a peevish whine. "I've got much more important things to do than standing here gabbing with you. Since you obviously aren't interested in caring for my horse, I'll go along and make other arrangements. So if you will kindly step aside . . ."

"Oh, no, you don't," Muggins snapped. "Now that you've seen what you've seen and shot off your mouth, the only way you'll go outa here is in a box." He glared past the hunter's shoulder. "You took your goddam time gettin' down here, Ox. Now move in careful and get his gun. It'll be somewhere underneath that crazy nightshirt getup."

Behind the hunter a new voice said, "Well, hell, George, I hadda put on my pants an' shirt, di'n' I?"

The hunter looked over his shoulder. The aptly named Ox was closing in behind him with exaggerated stealth, in the process of clumsily switching his gun from his right to his left hand. For the instant, neither hand held the gun in firing position.

The hunter spun around, gambling that the other two

would know a moment's hesitation in firing directly
toward their colleague. His shoulder rammed the big
man's midsection like a battering ram, driving the breath
from his lungs. At the same instant he grabbed the two
huge wrists and yanked with all his might.

The hulking Ox was hurled forward and in front as
both Ike and George broke the momentary paralysis and
fired. The hunter could hear the *thwuck-thwuck!* of the
slugs slamming into the spinning body, which served as his
own fleeting shield.

Then his own gun was in his hand and blasting thunder-
ously in the echoing gloom. Ike and George were both
dead an instant before the whirling body of Ox slammed
into them and carried them down with him in a charnel
heap.

The hunter waited, his cocked gun ready. The horses
were dancing and snorting, hauling against their halter
ropes. But there were no sounds, either from the hayloft
overhead or from below to indicate that the shots had
brought anyone else. He reloaded, then cautiously moved
forward.

The big moon face of the third man rang no cash
register bell in his memory. Apparently the Ox was either
too new or too inept at outlawry to rate a bounty notice.
Oh well, the hunter reflected, you can't win 'em all, and
twelve-fifty isn't too bad for a few moments of violence.

He dragged the bodies into a small feed room, half-
filled with sacks of oats and cracked corn, and eased
himself back outside. The ghost town of Spondulix was
still empty and quiet, drowsing in the memories of its
lively past. The brief thunder of gunfire had stirred only
the pack rats and the ghosts.

He mounted and rode out of town, following a deep-
rutted road that was only visible at intervals between
drifts of sand. The road led to a huddle of unpainted
buildings clustered close to the base of *E-Wai-Yah,* the
Spirit Mountain of the Indians, the massive, flat-sided rock
the owners of Spondulix had enthusiastically dubbed a
"Mountain of Gold."

He rode past signs reading PRIVATE PROPERTY—KEEP
OUT and TRESPASSERS WILL BE PROSECUTED. Someone with
more imagination had added a more recent sign: NOT
RESPONSIBLE FOR INJURIES OR DEATHS DUE TO GUNFIRE!

The mine office with its faded, almost undecipherable

sign had a shuttered, abandoned appearance. So did the half-dozen sprawling equipment sheds and warehouses. But curiously, the rails of the narrow-gauge track disappearing into the mine entrance were shiny and free from the rust of abandonment.

As the hunter swung down from the saddle, two hard-faced guards stepped out of the mine entrance. Both wore handguns, with the tied-down holsters of professional gunslingers, and each had a rifle cradled in his arms. One was indisputably a wanted outlaw known as Red Buckley, worth twelve hundred dollars. The other, while unknown, was clearly cut to the same pattern.

"Now you've seen the Spondulix Mine," Red Buckley said without preamble, "so hoist your ass back onto the leather and get the hell out of here. Those signs you passed back there weren't put up just for decorations. This *is* private property and you *are* trespassing, so clear the hell out before we stop pretending you're just a numbskull who can't read."

"That's clever, Red," the hunter said, "real good, in fact. How long did it take you to memorize that little speech?"

"Why, damn you," Red howled, and started to grab for his gun.

His arm froze in mid-grab. The bounty hunter's hand had seemed to do no more than twitch but abruptly his gun was in his hand, cocked and pointing at Red's middle.

He said softly, "Go ahead. Go right ahead, Red. The instant your hand touches the butt of that gun, you're a dead man. And I'm twelve hundred dollars' richer. I'd like that."

The door of the shuttered mine office suddenly slammed and a white-haired man in an expensive broadcloth business suit came running down a well-beaten path. He ran between the bounty hunter and Red Buckley.

"Stop it, you two! Stop it this minute! You—put up that gun and try to act like a civilized human being."

The hunter let his weapon droop but he neither lowered the hammer nor stowed it away. He noticed that Red Buckley's hand had hastily whipped back from his gun.

"You talk big," he said, deliberately prodding, "but I don't see any credentials. When a wanted killer and outlaw like Red Buckley makes a play, I make mine. If you're his nursemaid, trot out your bottle of milk, mister."

"I'm Daniel Murthy, the manager of the Spondulix," the white-haired man said. "And I hire guards for their competence at the job, not for their social background. Since you are a trespasser, you must expect to be greeted as one. Now, if you have any genuine business here, state it."

"I wonder," the hunter said, "if *you* have any genuine business here. If this is a mine that produces all by itself, without the help of any miners, it's the kind of miracle that ought to be reported widely."

Murthy's face was as white as his hair. His eyes were wild.

He wet his lips and said, "I—I guess I have to tell you, but I'd appreciate it if you didn't spread it around. When the Spondulix was at its peak of production we didn't have sufficient milling facilities to handle all the ore. So we processed only the richest and stockpiled the second-grade ore in some abandoned stopes. Now a new cyanide refining process makes it profitable to work the lower-grade ore. We *have* located a rich new vein, but the cost of exposing it will be enormous. We hope to finance the reopening of the Spondulix with the low-grade ore."

"But why all the secrecy?" the hunter demanded.

"Because if certain stockholders knew we were making a profit, they would demand their share as dividends immediately instead of using it to finance future operations. Now if I've satisfied your curiosity, sir, I'd appreciate it if you'd keep it to yourself."

"I'll do that," the hunter said.

He swung into the saddle, included the trio in a flip of his hand and headed back in the direction of the ghost town and two corpses waiting to be converted into cash. As he rode he pondered what he had seen and heard. Two conclusions were uppermost in his mind. One of them was that, for whatever reason, Daniel Murthy was a badly frightened man. The second was that the mine manager was also a very poor liar.

No one in his right mind would ship unmilled ore by the boxful. He was familiar enough with mining to know that even with a rich vein, it would take more than three tons of ore to produce one ounce of refined gold. The amount of ore that could be packed in a Wells Fargo box would not yield enough metal to pay its shipping cost.

Only pure gold dust, nuggets or the refined metal would

be shipped in that manner. But neither the huge stamp mill that pulverized the ore nor the refinery that separated the gold from the crushed rock showed any indication of having been used since the mine closed.

There was, as Sheriff Dobrin had so aptly put it, something altogether fishy about the purported "reopening" of the Spondulix Mine.

Chapter 4

The Reverend Leemon Fairfeather re-added the column of figures for the fourth time and sighed deeply. No matter whether he started at the top and worked down, or at the bottom and worked up, the total still came out to only forty thousand dollars—ten thousand short of the promised bounty on The Man With No Name. Not that forty thousand was exactly a sack of corn shucks, but his mouth was made up for the full amount and he could almost taste the added luxuries which that ten thousand would buy.

That left him with only two alternatives, neither of them exactly pleasant to contemplate. He could work back northward, contacting outlaw groups until the balance of the reward had been pledged. But this would consume valuable time and meanwhile the bounty hunter would not be idle.

Here, in the midst of virgin territory, he would be pursuing his bloody trade with a vengeance. Some of the outlaws he would gun down would undoubtedly be those who had pledged major contributions to the reward fund. That would upset the whole carefully planned scheme. Equally unpleasant, he would be collecting bounties on them—bounties the Reverend Fairfeather had planned on collecting for himself as soon as the fifty thousand was safely in his hand.

The second alternative was not only unpleasant but involved a high element of personal risk. According to fairly dependable rumor, Blood Hand, the renegade Chiricahua Apache, had begun to admit white savages as well as half-breeds to his growing army of plunderers. His forays had taken on more the aspect of bandit raids than Indian attacks, evidence of growing white influence. The bounty on his head was growing to astronomical proportions and it was only a matter of time until the more daring bounty hunters set out to collect it. Given the right approach, Bloody Hand might be amenable to putting up the balance of the blood money on the bounty hunter's head.

The Reverend Fairfeather sighed deeply. He opened the pseudo-Bible and carefully checked the shells and the hammer-action on the long-barreled pistol clipped inside. Satisfied but far from happy, he replaced the gun, closed the cover and swung out of the saddle. Laying the book aside he pulled a rawhide thong holding what appeared to be his bedroll tied on the saddle skirt.

The blanket unrolled with a snap, revealing a lining of canvas to which were clipped a high-powered lever-action rifle and a double-barreled shotgun. He checked the loads in both, then rerolled the pack and secured it again with the thong. Clutching the book, he remounted and turned the mule's head in the direction of Dollar Sign Canyon.

At the top of the ridge the bounty hunter halted to light one of his stubby *cigarros*. Under cover of the act he looked back at the building clustered around the mine head. The three men had disappeared, the guards probably back inside the mine shaft and Murthy into his boarded-up office. The property once more took on the appearance of abandonment, desolation and decay.

Below the crest and out of sight of the mine, the hunter swung off the trail toward a grove of trees. Leaving his horse where it would not be visible from the trail, he got a collapsible spy glass out of a saddlebag and climbed back up the ridge on foot.

At the top he bellied down in the shadow of a rock, adjusted the glass and studied the scene he had just left. There was no movement, no sign of life. He was settl'ng down for what might well be a long wait when Red Buckley came around a corner of the stamp mill leading a saddled horse. He left the horse in front of the mine office and went inside. After perhaps ten minutes or so he came out again, swinging a pair of saddlebags that appeared to be empty. He draped these across the horse's withers and swung into the saddle.

Instead of taking the trail to Spondulix, however, he headed straight south. Through his glass the bounty hunter could see that Red was following what appeared to be a thread of well-beaten trail. He scowled in puzzlement. As he remembered from earlier travels, there was nothing in that direction but mountainous, virtually impassable wilderness, slashed across by the awesome chasm of Dollar Sign Canyon. What possible excuse there could be for traffic heavy enough to beat a trail only added one more facet to the mystery of the Spondulix Mine.

He got his horse and struck out in pursuit, making a broad detour that struck the mysterious trail some two miles below the mine. A line of fresh hoof prints was already beginning to fill with wind-blown sand, indicating that the outlaw must be at least a mile further along the trail.

As he rode, the hunter tucked his poncho aside and loosened his gun in its holster. A short way ahead, he remembered, the trail would plunge into an area labeled on maps as The Giants. These were massive rock formations carved into grotesque shapes by wind and weather and strewn so thickly throughout the region that an army could find easy concealment.

If, the hunter mused grimly, the Good Lord had not intended men to ambush one another, He would have had no excuse whatever for creating The Giants.

So far, he had caught no glimpse of Red Buckley on the trail ahead. But that was no assurance whatever that Red had not caught a glimpse of him.

The Reverend Fairfeather had had several sound reasons for selecting a mule instead of a horse as his mount. For one thing, he fancied a mule lent a subtle suggestion of humility to his masquerade. His other reasons were the more practical ones that led many experienced frontiersmen and even veteran U.S. Cavalry troopers to prefer mules over horses.

A mule had a rougher, less comfortable gait than a horse but greater endurance and, except for its unpredictable moods of stubbornness, greater docility. More important, while Indians would go to any length to steal a horse, they generally despised and even feared mules. Many an immigrant train had escaped attack by switching from horses or oxen to mules at the border of Indian country.

But most important of all, mules were far less liable to be panicked at the rank animal smell of the red man. Horses, on the other hand, could be stampeded by the mere scent of Indians drifting to them downwind. The Indians were well aware of this equine characteristic and used it frequently and with great success in their attacks on whites. A few years later they would employ it to stampede the horses of the Seventh Cavalry, stranding General Custer and his troopers on the blood-soaked hillside where they died to the last man.

Nevertheless, the nerves of even the most phlegmatic mule have their limits. As the Reverend Fairfeather's mount jogged in through the gloomy portals of Dollar Sign Canyon, the animal began to show every evidence of strain and fright. His gait slowed to a stumbling walk and his big ears whipped back and forth like semaphores wig-wagging a message of disaster. He kept tugging at the reins, trying to turn his head far enough to look behind.

The Reverend Fairfeather addressed him in Biblical language taken somewhat out of context, but the result was only increased nervousness on the part of the animal.

"Dammit to hell," the Reverend raged. "Quiet down and stop fancy-dancing all over the place. I'm trying to concentrate on what I'll say to Bloody Hand first thing when we meet. If I don't say the right things and say them fast, neither one of us will get out of here alive."

The mule suddenly snorted, threw up its head and stopped so abruptly that its rider was almost pitched forward onto its neck. A dozen feet in front, an Indian sat on a spotted pony, blocking the narrow trail.

He had the fierce, hawk-nosed features and squat, barrel-chested figure of the typical Apache. His costume consisted of moccasins, breechclout and headband and a multicolored coat of war paint. His appearance was altogether savage and primitive—but there was nothing primitive about the Sharps carbine he was pointing at the Reverend Fairfeather's chest.

The Reverend forced a smile and started to lift his hand, palm out, in a gesture of peace. At that moment the mule uttered a high-pitched squawl and bucked so violently that its rider had all he could do to hang onto the Bible, the reins and the saddlehorn all at the same time.

He was so preoccupied with keeping his seat that he never saw the second Indian who had stepped out onto the trail behind him and who stopped jabbing his scalping knife into the mule's buttock long enough to step forward

and smash his war club onto the back of the Reverend
Fairfeather's skull.

The bounty hunter's observation post was the flat top of
one of the Giants—a sixty-foot column of sandstone tor-
mented into obscene shape by time and the elements. It
was not only one of the tallest in the vicinity but it offered
natural footholds and handholds that made climbing it
relatively easy.

From this elevation he could look east and west across
untold miles of similar formations crowded along a relatively narrow strip of ground, paralleling the rim of Dollar
Sign Canyon. He could even see past the rim of the
canyon, less than a half-mile south, into the upper reaches
of the gloomy gorge. In the opposite direction a sharp
outcropping of rock formed a natural wall that marked
the northern boundary of The Giants.

Almost underneath his perch, at the base of the outcropping, Red Buckley's horse still waited patiently, tethered in a narrow passage between massive rocks. A quar-
ter-mile or so back and some two hundred yards off the
trail, the hunter's own horse was similarly concealed.

He had been close enough to see Red stake his mount
and go scrambling up over the rock outcropping, carrying
his empty saddlebags. By the time he got there, however,
the outlaw had lost himself in the maze of rock formations beyond the wall. Since Red Buckley seemed the most
available key to the Spondulix mystery, he had found, and
scrambled to the top of, The Giant. With luck he would
spot Red returning to his horse and get at least a general
idea of the area he had visited.

He leveled his spyglass, cupping his hand above the end
so that no reflected beam of sunlight, striking from the
lens or the brass fitting, would give him away. Searching
the most likely areas where Red might have vanished, he
could see no sign of life or movement.

Then, quite suddenly, Red was there, coming around
the base of a sandstone column. His thin, sallow face, with
its mass of freckles and thicket of sandy whiskers, swam
into his field of vision. The saddlebags slung over his right
shoulder were no longer empty but bulging with something
so heavy it dragged his shoulder down and gave him an
awkward lopsided gait.

The hunter dropped the glass and snatched his gun.

Using his left arm for a rest he trained it on the man below, following his stumbling progress. If Red had glanced upward at any time, he would have been a dead man, but he was too preoccupied with his burden and his footing. He lowered himself gingerly over the outcropping and draped the saddlebags across the cantle of his saddle.

When the outlaw had vanished up the trail back to the Spondulix, the hunter stowed away his gun and spyglass and worked his way down to the ground. He had marked in his mind's eye the spot where Red had made his sudden reappearance and he found his way to it quickly.

He reached the precise point where the outlaw had stumbled into view around the sandstone column, only to encounter another exercise in frustration. Red could have reached there by any one of a dozen narrow, meandering pathways that fanned out among the sandstone columns. There was nothing different to see, no clue of any kind. The ground was mainly rock on which no boot prints could show.

He chose a direction at random and followed it as far as the lapsed time indicated Red could have gone for his mysterious burden. Nowhere along the route could he see a trace of digging or any other human activity. He made his way back to his starting point and tried another wandering corridor with the same negative result.

In time he lost count of the number of false trails he had patiently explored. He was trudging back from another failure when a wisp of vagrant breeze touched his skin with a moment's coolness. For the briefest of instants his nostrils caught the unmistakable aroma of roasting meat. It was gone almost before his mind identified the scent and the air was once more still and hot.

He stood rigid, sniffing, trying to reconstruct the moment in his mind. He was almost certain the breeze had struck his left cheek. He wet a forefinger and held it up. A faint coolness on the side toward the air movement confirmed the direction.

He cat-footed in that direction with his hand on his gun, his nostrils flaring and every sense doubly alert. His course took him toward a truncated column whose entire upper section appeared to have been blasted off by a lightning bolt in some ancient past. Great chunks of shattered sandstone, some as big as a small cabin, had been flung around its base. As the hunter approached the jum-

ble of rocks the aroma of cooking again reached his
nostrils, stronger this time and not dependent upon the
breeze to waft it.

The mysterious cookfire was almost surely somewhere
among those fallen rocks. That meant that somewhere
there had to be a passage between the rocks, since nothing
short of a mountain goat could clamber over them. The
hunter drew his gun and began warily to skirt the perime-
ter of the pile.

He wormed his way into several narrow spaces that
looked promising, only to have them dead-end abruptly or
squeeze down to impassable slits. Then, at long last, he
tried one that widened instead of narrowing as he wormed
his way inward. The scent of roasting meat was very
strong and mingled with it was the odor of freshly baked
bread. The smells made the hunter's mouth water and his
stomach grumble a reminder that it was now nearing
sundown and he had eaten nothing since dawn.

The passageway bent sharply around another fallen
rock, then abruptly opened onto a relatively clear space in
the midst of the rockfall. The bounty hunter thumbed
back the hammer of his gun and cautiously peered out.
The clearing was roughly circular, perhaps a hundred feet
in diameter, the ground littered with boulders and fragments of shattered sandstone.

The aroma of cooking hung heavily in the clearing, but
nowhere could he see a sign of life or a trace of a
cookfire. He was staring around, completely baffled, when
a hollow, disembodied voice boomed out of nowhere.

"All right, you rannies," the voice said, sounding like an
echo of itself. "Grub's on. Come and get it or I'll throw it
away."

At the first sound of a human voice, the hunter took a
quick step backward, away from the mouth of the passage. He backed into something round and hard that
jabbed just beneath his left shoulder blade.

At his shoulder a voice that was anything but disembodied rasped harshly, "Hold it, snooper! You worked so
hard getting this far, you might as well go the rest of the
way. Start walkin' straight ahead and don't try any
tricks."

A hand reached past him and roughly snatched away
his gun.

Chapter 5

The Reverend Leemon Fairfeather was having a nightmare, a fearfully bad nightmare—as if there could ever be such a thing as a good nightmare. But this one exceeded all the limits of reason in its horror.

In the dream he had been running, running, with a blood-maddened mountain lion bounding in slavering pursuit. For moments it almost seemed that he might outdistance the beast and escape. Perhaps he would have—if he hadn't tripped over an exposed tree root and slammed down on his face, the breath all knocked out of his lungs.

Before he could move, the lion was on his back, clawing savagely, ripping shirt and flesh. He wanted to yell with the agony of it but something told him he must keep his lips sealed at all costs. He tried to roll away from the beast's ripping claws, to fend it off somehow, but his arms and, in fact, his entire body was completely paralyzed. Not a single muscle would respond to his anguished mental commands.

Then, after an eternity of pain, he somehow forced his eyes to open. The dream vanished but not the agony. His back was still being cruelly lacerated and his body and arms were still immobile, but looking down, he understood the reason. It was still a nightmare, but no longer a dream.

He was seated on the ground, naked to the waist. His arms were tightly bound to his sides by a broad belt of rawhide. A second strip of rawhide encircled his chest and upper arms just below his shoulders.

Without looking, he knew that the rawhide was green, just cut from the hide of a freshly-killed beef animal. He knew as surely that the strips bound him to a huge barrel cactus whose vicious barbed spines were digging into his naked back.

This was the favorite Apache form of torture, supposedly invented by them and dreaded by every white person on the frontier. As the green rawhide dried under the blazing sun, it shrank, drawing the helpless victim ever tighter against the cruel spines. After an interminable period, the victim would finally be released from his agony when the cactus spines reached a vital organ.

The Reverend Fairfeather painfully raised his head. The savages were there, some thirty of them, all fiercely painted and armed with an assortment of both ancient and modern weapons. They were sitting in a semi-circle, watching him. Their dark, hawkish faces were impassive but their eyes glittered with anticipation of the moment when he would begin to scream. The squat figure of Bloody Hand himself sat a little ahead of the others.

The tortured man set his jaw to bite back a groan. As he regained control, he began to speak but his voice came out in the guttural staccato of the Chiricahua Apache dialect.

"What is this?" he managed between spasms of pain. "Is this how the noted Bloody Hand greets a blood brother who has come to offer good tidings?"

There was a murmur of astonishment among the seated members of the band. Bloody Hand had leaped to his feet. For a moment, the much-vaunted Indian stoicism of countenance gave way to open shock.

"You—you Anglo! You speak perfectly the tongue of the Chiricahua Apache. What trick is this?"

"Why shouldn't I speak it?" the Reverend Fairfeather managed. "My mother was a Jicarillo Apache. When I was a small child, my father returned to his estates in Germany and my mother took me to live in the lodge of a Chiricahua man. I grew up among your people. Although my blood is part Jicarillo, my knowledge of their dialect is but poor."

"It is a trick," Bloody Hand raged. "It must be a trick. If you are truly Apache, tell me—what is your Indian name?"

The Reverend Fairfeather fought to suppress another moan. The rawhide was inexorably tightening, the agony growing more intense.

"My baby name," he managed, "in Jicarillo I was too young to know. But in Chiricahua it was Hon-dah—welcome to this house. This was the name by which I was known until my youth when I went alone into the moun-

tains and captured a golden eagle, from whom I plucked
the gorgeous tail fathers for my medicine bonnet.
Thereafter, I was known as Golden Feather. At the Anglo
mission school where I was sent they translated my name
as Fairfeather. So I am now called the Reverend Leemon
Fairfeather."

"Reverend?" Bloody Hand growled. "An Anglo priest?"
He tramped to where the mule was tethered nearby, still
bridled and saddled, its rump caked with dried blood. A
jerk of the thong and the blanket unrolled, exposing the
rifle and shotgun. "Then how do you explain these, Reverend?"

The Man With No Name stumbled across the rock-
strewn clearing, kept off-balance by vicious jabs of the gun
muzzle. The odor of food mingled with that of a wood fire
was almost overpowering, but there was still no visible
indication of its source. This, he reflected grimly, could be
called solving mysteries the hard way.

"Around behind that rock," his captor growled. "The
big one straight ahead."

The bounty hunter rounded the rock and stopped so
suddenly that his captor's gun rammed painfully into his
back. The answer to at least one mystery lay almost at his
feet.

It was a broad fissure, a crack in the bedrock caused by
some ancient upheaval. From this issued the odors of
food, an almost-invisible thread of wood smoke and the
unmistakable murmur of men's voices. The voices had a
hollow ring that suggested they were coming from a
sizeable cavern deep in the bowels of the earth.

The bounty hunter's captor edged cautiously around
him and into view for the first time. He was a long,
cadaverous figure with the stooped shoulders and caved-in
chest of a tubercular and a shock of hair so blond it
bordered on albino white. Keeping his gun trained steadily
on his prisoner, he squatted down by the fissure and
bawled, *"Canuse! Hey, Canuse!"*

The murmur of voices broke off, then a single male
voice boomed hollowly from below.

"Pinky? What the hell you doin' back here? You're
supposed to be out watchin' the slot."

"I *was* watching it. That's how come I caught us a
visitor prowlin' around up here without no invite. I'm

sendin' him down first. You fellers cover him from down there."

In response to a sharp gesture, the hunter stepped to the crack. A sturdy wooden ladder, bolted to the rock side, led down into blackness. At the base of the blackness, perhaps fifty feet down, was a circle of faint light.

The voice below boomed, "Okay, you can start him down, now. We're ready for him. And tell him to be careful on the ladder. We wouldn't want a guest to have an accident."

"You heard him," Pinky snarled. *"Move!"*

The bounty hunter swung himself onto the ladder and began a cautious descent. Up above, Pinky stood framed in the fissure, his gun poised and ready. He was not about to start down and get caught in a blast of gunfire from below in case his prisoner made any overt moves to draw shots from those at the bottom of the shaft. The hunter had a momentary impulse to use one of his hidden derringers on the silhouette above, but it would serve no purpose and the falling body of Pinky could sweep him off the ladder to his death, or into the hands of the gang below, which could prove equally lethal.

The fissure narrowed until for some distance his back was brushing the opposite wall, then widened again until he stepped off the bottom of the ladder into a large deep-shadowed cavern. A wood fire was burning in the center of the rock floor, the shaft serving as a natural chimney to dissipate its thin smoke. The light of the fire was augmented by a coal oil lantern but much of the cavern remained in deep shadow.

Meat was sizzling on a spit over the fire and a chipped enamel coffee pot steamed on the embers. A long rope of dough, coiled around a second spit was being half baked and half scorched into bread. Ranged on the floor by the fire were six tin plates bearing the remains of the interrupted meal.

The six owners of the plates were fanned out facing the ladder, guns in hand. They were a uniformly hard-bitten lot, although none of them registered in the bounty hunter's mental catalog of wanted men. A big man, a shade cleaner than his companions and wearing a subtle air of authority, studied the hunter through narrowed eyes and nodded.

"Yep, it's him, all right. The bounty killer with no

name. The one they call Mister Sudden Death. I figured as much when Red described the fella snooping around the mine."

Pinky came clattering down the ladder, grinning broadly.

"How was that for a nice haul, Canuse? I did all right, nailin' him, didn't I?"

"You're great, Pinky," the big man said dryly. "Give yourself a nice pat on the back, then get the hell back to the slot before somebody else comes nosing in."

Pinky's grin faded.

"Aw, have a heart, Canuse, and send one of the others up for a while. I already been on watch for hours and I'm so dang starved my stomach thinks my throat's been cut."

"You heard me," Canuse said harshly. "Get going or maybe your throat will get cut." He held out his free hand. "Leave his gun with me. I'll take good care of it."

Pinky pulled the hunter's gun from his belt and reluctantly surrendered it. He turned and went up the ladder with dragging steps, muttering to himself. Canuse tucked the hunter's gun into his own belt. He gestured toward a small, thin man.

"Sag, go get the longest rawhide thong you can find to tie this ranny up. Try to get one long enough to tie his ankles and wrists together."

"Aw, why don't we just plug the bastard and get back to our supper before it's burnt all to hell?"

"Because I want some answers before we finish him off," Canuse's voice rose to a bellow. "And because I told you what to do. Go do it!"

"Awright, awright," the little man said. He grabbed the lantern and vanished into what appeared to be a passage off the main cavern.

"How'd you find this place?" Canuse demanded, swinging back to the hunter. "By following Red here?"

"By following my nose," the hunter said. "I picked up the smell of your roast a good mile away, downwind. Does your big boss know how stupidly careless you are?"

Canuse turned a deep crimson. He cursed the hunter in a thick, choked voice.

"Goddam your soul, I'm the boss."

"You? Don't make me laugh. Whoever planned this little game had a *few* brains—except when it came to picking his helpers."

"Go ahead," the big man raged. "Keep it up. Have your fun now while you can. Because in about two shakes you're all finished, Mr. Sudden Death. That name is going to fit you like a glove."

A stocky man with an ugly, knife-scarred face growled, "Any time you want him plugged, Canuse, just say the word."

"I wouldn't waste a bullet on him. We'll toss him off the ledge and let the damn Cherry Cows down there go crazy trying to figure where the mess came from."

The small, thin Sag came back. He set the lantern down on the floor and held up a bundle of leather thongs, each no more than six or seven inches in length.

"If there's any rawhide longer'n these, I sure as hell can't find 'em. Maybe you forgot you had us cut 'em all to this length for tyin' up the pokes."

"The great brain," the hunter murmured audibly.

Canuse whirled, his face nearly purple with fury. He pointed his gun at the hunter's chest, his hand shaking with the effort to control his murderous rage.

"Damn you, damn you, damn you!" he cried in a strangled voice. "Keep it up! Keep on asking for it, you cute-mouth sonuvabitch! I want to know what you're nosin' around our business for in the first place and I want a straight answer. You got no concern with whatever we're doing."

"Just curious, that's all," the hunter said, elaborately stifling an artificial yawn. "I'm curious about why a man like Murthy should act scared half to death, or why he'd turn into a lousy liar about a business he knows like the palm of his hand. Or how a mine can produce a boxful of pure gold every week without a miner in the shafts, or a stamp mill or refinery in operation."

"What the hell's it to *you?*" Canuse yelled. "Your trade is hunting down outlaws with bounties on their heads. So what the hell should you mess with our business for?"

"Because," the bounty hunter said blandly, "when I encounter a scheme like this, I know the people I hunt down are somewhere behind it, so when I trace it to the top, I'll have me a fine lot of lovely bounties."

He emphasized his remarks with gestures of his right hand, while his left hand slipped from view under the tail of the poncho. His deliberate attempt to goad Canuse into rash action had reached and passed its objective. From here on life balanced on the thinnest of barricades.

"Grab him!" Canuse yelled. "That's enough out of him. Tie one of those thongs around each wrist and then tie the two thongs together so it's like handcuffs. Hurry up, you dummies! Don't just stand there."

"No," the hunter said. "Don't just stand there. Lie down and roll on the floor."

He brought his left hand around, holding the double-barreled derringer with the huge bore. His first shot went into the heart of the fire, sending a cloud of burning embers and wood fragments flying over and onto the gang. The slug ricocheted from the rock floor and lifted a second cloud, scattering most of the fire over the howling group.

His shot from the second barrel took Canuse squarely between the eyes.

The big man was still falling when the hunter dived and snatched his gun from the other's belt. He landed on his shoulder, rolled and came up fanning the hammer of the deadly forty-four. The five had their guns out but at the moment they were dancing, howling, rolling, beating at the flames started in their clothing or branded into exposed flesh by the flying embers.

The shots made one deafening crescendo in the confines of the echoing cavern. When the echoes had finally died, the hunter got warily to his feet. The caution was needless. Six hardcases would never again be a menace to anyone on this earth.

He reloaded his gun, then stood utterly motionless, barely breathing, for dragging minutes. He had no way of knowing how extensive the caverns and tunnels might be, or whether or not other bands might be bivouacked near enough to be drawn by the shots.

When there was no rush of footsteps or any whisper of sound, he turned and went to the base of the ladder, looking up. High above, a rough circle framed a patch of brilliant, cerulean-blue evening sky. He waited with his gun poised, expecting at any moment to see the silhouette of Pinky's head and shoulders move into the frame.

When no figure appeared after an interminable wait, he holstered his gun and backed away from the ladder. Probably the racketing gunfire had been too muffled by the depth of the cavern to reach the lookout's post. Nevertheless, he kept every sense alert on the off-chance that there might be another entrance Pinky could use to surprise him.

He turned up the wick of the lantern for maximum illumination and held it above eye level as he peered around. Seen in brighter light, the cavern proved much smaller than it had appeared at first. It contained, besides the cookfire and its late patrons, nothing but a row of yellow oilskins hanging from pegs beside the ladder.

A large, irregular blotch of deeper blackness opposite the ladder marked the passageway where Sag had gone in search of the rawhide thong. At right angles to it, a second and somewhat larger blotch marked the entrance to a converging passageway. The bounty hunter flipped a mental coin and selected the smaller passage for his first exploration.

He was at the entrance when the voice of Pinky echoed down the shaft. "Canuse! Oh, Canuse! Goddammit, I'm not stayin' out there any longer. It's getting so dark I couldn't see a herd of elephants from the lookout, anyhow, and my gut is screamin' at me, it's so goddam empty."

The hunter set down the lantern, cupped a hand in front of his mouth and shouted, "All right! Come on down, then."

He waited, empty hands relaxed at his sides. Heavy boots squealed and thudded on the rungs of the ladder. The lower part of Pinky's elongated structure came into view, followed finally by the shock of pale blond hair. He came down grumbling audibly.

"Goddamndest way to treat a man, Canuse! I work my ass off on the vein, then I go out there and put in three-four hours broiling on that lookout point and then. . . ."

He reached the last rung, jumped off, started to turn and froze, gaping at the sprawled corpse of Canuse which was nearest the ladder. From just beyond his range of vision the hunter said softly, *"Bang-Bang!* You're dead!"

Pinky's head swiveled far enough to take in the remaining bodies and the poncho-draped figure of their killer standing with empty hands hanging loose and easy at his sides. Pinky's jaw dropped and his eyes went wide and wild.

He made the fatal mistake of going for his gun.

Chapter 6

The green rawhide straps were steadily shrinking, shrinking, drawing the naked back of the Reverend Leemon Fairfeather ever tighter against the spines of the cactus to which he was bound. The agony was excruciating, but his only hope of escape was to convince Bloody Hand, the Chiricahua Apache chief, that he, too, was part Apache. To do that he must display the stoicism of the Indian at all costs.

"Answer me, Reverend," Bloody Hand spat again, slapping the fake bedroll with the shotgun and the high-power rifle clipped to the canvas lining. "If you are truly the Anglo priest, as you claim, explain why you are secretly carrying these weapons."

The Reverend Fairfeather fought down another spasm of acute pain and gasped, "To kill varmints. They are many and dangerous along the lonely trails I travel and not all of them are the four-legged kind. I have sometimes found it necessary to kill the two-legged ones who would prey on me or on my people ... who are also your people." He turned his head to keep pace with the back-and-forth tramping of Bloody Hand, but the effort, the straining of tissues and moving of muscles, was almost beyond endurance. The viciously barbed cactus spines were digging deeper and ever deeper into the flesh of his back. His chances of surviving the traditional Apache torture ordeal were diminishing by the minute.

"*My* people," Bloody Hand sneered. "Who are *my* people? *My* people are those you see before you here."

"They—are the ones—I mean. See paper—in—saddle-bag."

The Reverend Fairfeather's senses were reeling. The stocky figure of Bloody Hand swam in and out of focus as the Apache rummaged in the saddlebag. There was a rustle of paper and a distinctly un-Indian grunt of surprise.

"You—Cut-Lip," the guttural voice of Bloody Hand called. "Read this paper and tell what marching sticks say."

"Sure, chief," a rough American voice said. "Hell, I know who this hombre is. He's the bounty killer they call The Man With No Name and Mister Sudden Death. He's bad medicine for any outlaw with a price on his head. I've seen his gun-work and I wouldn't trade lead with him for all the gold in the Rockies." He laboriously stumbled through the bounty poster, struggling hopelessly with any words of more than one syllable. "Hell, chief, if I was you I'd peel that feller off the cactus and keep him alive till we find out what he knows about this deal and where he fits into the picture."

The Reverend Fairfeather was mercifully unconscious when they tore his bloody back loose from the impaling cactus spines.

The passageway took an abrupt turn and widened into a second cavern that appeared to have been the living quarters for the defunct crew. The bounty hunter held the lantern high, studying the room for some clue to whatever mysterious operation they had been conducting.

Eight bunks stood along one side of the cavern in four double tiers. A long board studded with wooden pegs held a row of spare shirts, long johns and fancy vests. Other items of clothing and personal effects were stowed under the lower tier of bunks in cardboard suitcases and carpetbags. At one end of the bunks a crude shelf held a row of shaving mugs and brushes with straight razors folded beside each. A small, cracked mirror hung from the footboard of the upper bunk.

The wall opposite the bunks was piled high with staple supplies. There were sacks of flour, small casks of sugar, a stack of smoke-cured bacon sides, a barrel of soda crackers, cases of canned peaches.

The hunter lifted the lid of an unmarked case and whistled softly. Stacked inside were literally hundreds of empty buckskin pouches or "pokes" of the type commonly used as purses or for packing gold dust. Packed with them was a bundle of short rawhide thongs to be threaded through slits at the top of each poke to form drawstrings.

He nodded grimly. The discovery supplied some small confirmation of a theory that had been taking shape in his mind.

There appeared to be nothing else of immediate significance and he was suddenly on fire with eagerness to investigate the other, larger passageway. He paused in the entrance cavern to look regretfully at the sprawled corpses. Although obviously of the outlaw breed, none of them registered in his mind as having a bounty on his head. In his cash register system of reckoning, their demise was a sheer waste of bullets.

He had wanted at least one of them alive and in condition to clear up some of the mysteries, but they had forced his hand. Their rashness had left him no alternative except to kill or be killed. He sighed heavily and turned to the larger passage.

Before he had taken a half-dozen steps he had full confirmation of his theory and the answers to at least a part of the mystery of the Spondulix Mine. The left-hand wall of the passage had a deep horizontal channel gouged out of the rock. The channel was roughly shoulder high, although it veered up and down somewhat. The floor at the base of the wall was littered with rock chips.

Even before he held the lantern high for a closer look, he was sure what he would see, but he was not prepared for the magnitude of his discovery. The channel itself and the surrounding rock were thickly veined with threads of pure gold. These had originally radiated from the main body of the vein, which had been gouged out, forming the channel. It must have been fantastically rich for the operator to leave behind threads of gold that would be considered a major strike in the average mine.

The further the hunter moved along the passageway, the thicker grew the network of remaining veins. With proper milling and extraction methods those golden threads could still yield a modest fortune. And this was only the surface metal. There was no guessing how deep into the rock the hairline threads might run.

Abruptly he came upon the site of current operations. A row of heavy iron spikes or bolts had been driven high in the wall. Lanterns were hung from these with reflectors adjusted to focus the light on the main gold vein. The bounty hunter threw his own light on the untouched portion of the vein and sucked in a sharp breath. It was

no wonder the operator was willing to leave a small
fortune in thread-size veins behind. Sections of the main
ore body were pipes of pure gold as thick as a man's
upper arm.

An assortment of heavy mining tools was lined against
the opposite wall. A little further along, a barrel reeking
of coal oil was elevated on rocks so that the lanterns could
be filled directly from the spigot.

The sound of splashing water drew the hunter on a few
additional steps. The water was coming through cracks in
the rock ceiling, probably from an underground spring,
and trickling down the wall into a small natural catch
basin at the foot. A wooden bucket of water stood beside
the basin and a tin dipper hung from a spike wedged into
a crack in the rock. The water was sweet and cold enough
to make the teeth ache.

A dozen yards beyond the spring the lantern light fell
on what appeared to be the abrupt end of the passageway.
As he approached it, however, the hunter discovered it
was actually a curtain of gray canvas concealing the
mouth of the passageway. He left the lantern on the rock
floor a good twenty feet back and twitched the edge of
the canvas aside just far enough to peer out.

He was looking toward a segment of the Southwest sky,
ablaze with the final riot of sunset colors. Beneath this was
a vast sea of blackness that could only be the huge
Dollar-Sign Canyon, in whose depths nightfall came early.
A cluster of tiny flickering sparks far below would be the
night fires of the marauding Apaches who had seized the
canyon and claimed it for their own.

The hunter let the canvas drop back into place and took
up the lantern. As he raised it, the light fell on a wooden
chest previously hidden in the shadow of the coal oil
barrel. Made of unpainted wood, it was roughly the size
and shape of the gray treasure boxes carried on Wells-
Fargo coaches. He raised the lid and sucked in another
sharp breath.

The box was half-filled with buckskin pokes, all full of
some substance, the drawstrings tied. He knew even before he hefted the first poke what its contents would be.
He untied the drawstring and poured out a palmful of
fragments and particles of pure raw gold.

He studied it, scowling, then poured it back and retied
the poke. He rocked back on his heels, lit one of the small

cigarros and pieced together the facts he had uncovered so far.

The chest of gold that was being shipped to the U.S. mint each Wednesday from the Spondulix Mine surely originated here, not in their empty, echoing stopes. The gold reached the Spondulix in the saddlebags of couriers like Red Buckley, a clumsy system but one far less conspicuous than a freight wagon. The mining method, though primitive and wasteful, must be immensely profitable. This was surely one of the richest lodes the West had ever revealed.

But the few answers only raised new and more baffling questions. Why the elaborate ruse to conceal the true origin of the gold? It would be simpler and far more economical simply to register this mine and proceed to work it openly with the latest tools and methods. Why was Murthy, the superintendent of the Spondulix, a desperately frightened man as well as a bad liar? And above all, who was the master mind behind this fantastic scheme?

The colorful blanket, procured from the neighboring Navajos either by theft or, less likely, trade, was stretched on the floor of the big cave at the foot of the south wall of Dollar-Sign Canyon. The Reverend Leemon Fairfeather lay belly-down on the blanket, his upper torso raised on his naked elbows. His bare back, streaked with rivulets of dried blood and speckled with ragged openings where the cactus spines had torn free, glistened with a salve of bear grease and herbs the old women of the band had smeared on it. The herbs seemed to have some miraculous analgesic quality because the agony in his back had subsided to a tingling numbness.

He watched with narrowed wary eyes as Bloody Hand paced the confines of the cave like a penned tiger. Although he had been abruptly freed from the cactus torture and his torn back soothed with ointments, he had no illusion that he was safely past the danger point. The Apache was still a savage and unpredictable animal whose sole motivation would always be his own self-interest.

Bloody Hand paused in his pacing to glare at the reward poster from the Reverend Fairfeather's saddlebag. Looking beyond the squat figure, the Reverend could see the early shadows deepening in the canyon. The women were already bringing armloads of mesquite and paloverde and great pads of buffalo chips to build up the ring of cookfires. Midway up the opposite cliff the rays of the setting sun threw the mysterious dollar sign into sharp relief against the gray rock.

"This man," Bloody Hand rasped, slapping the poster with the back of his hand, "you say he is here somewhere now, and will come to kill me? Ho! Many, many men have tried to kill Bloody Hand and you can see how dead he is."

"I can see how dead he *might* be soon," the Reverend said grimly. "You may not know it but your price is going up. The bounty on your head was fifteen thousand dollars, and that is not exactly horse droppings. But after your bloody raid on Conche Springs a couple of weeks ago, the ante went up to twenty thousand. That's five thousand additional reasons for a bounty killer to take greater risks to get you. It might even be enough to make one of your own pack turn on you."

For a moment he thought Bloody Hand would kill him on the spot. The Apache's sullen face contorted in rage and his hand dropped to the hilt of the heavy scalping knife on his hip. He spat a stream of curses in a half-dozen Indian dialects until he ran out of breath. Then his rage died as suddenly as it had been born. His hand dropped from his knife and his face resumed its sullen mask.

He said, in a voice of reasonableness, "But I do not understand why I should help pay for the killing of this man if he is only one of dozens of bounty hunters."

"Because for one thing, my brother, he is more deadly dangerous than all those others together. For another, his rivals will be too busy trying for the fifty thousand dollars to bother with lesser bounties. You will all have easier hunting with less danger because of this. There will be so many bounty hunters stalking The Man With No Name that they will be falling over one another and killing one another in their jealous rivalry. Then he will kill the survivors in self-defense and soon he will be the only bounty hunter left."

"And then?"

"Then," the Reverend Fairfeather said smugly, "I shall kill the Nameless One and then there will be none."

"You are truly a Chiricahua Apache," Bloody Hand said. "Who else could think of such a fiendishly evil scheme? It is beautiful." He shook his head admiringly. "We will be glad to pay our share of the bounty . . ."

A shadow suddenly darkened the cave mouth. The Apache whirled in a half-crouch, his hand streaking to his knife. The Reverend Fairfeather gaped past him at a weird figure, who might have escaped from someone's nightmare.

The figure had once been a huge man, standing a good six feet seven or eight. Now he was a stooped and shrunken caricature of his own past, leaning on a shepherd's crook, so bent over that his vast tangle of dirty-white hair and beard nearly brushed the ground. His sole garment appeared to be a flowing robe that had once been white. On one foot he wore a thonged sandal and on the other an Indian moccasin, badly scuffed and missing most of its beadwork.

This could only be the character known as Herkimer the Mad Hermit, who occupied a barren cave in Dollar Sign Canyon. The Reverend Fairfeather had heard numerous stories about the old recluse, most of which were either wholly unbelievable or hopelessly conflicting.

In his more coherent moments Herkimer insisted that he was a hundred and nineteen years old and that as a boy he had witnessed the carving of the dollar sign on the cliff. He was the only living person, he swore, who knew *who* had done the carving and how and what the symbol's hidden message truly was. Unfortunately, when pressed for details he invariably drifted off into an utterly senseless babble that destroyed any credibility he might have won.

Yet it was this madness that had spared him from torture and death at the hands of the Indians. Many tribes held an insane person in superstitious awe as having been personally set apart from normal people by the Great Spirit. Even Bloody Hand, who had defied other superstitions, had bowed to this one and spared old Herkimer from the general massacre of white prospectors and treasure-seekers. Not only was he permitted to continue occupying his cave, but they kept him supplied with food.

Herkimer peered at the Apache and uttered a high, whinnying cackle of laughter.

"*Hee-hee-hee!* I spooked yuh good that time, didn't I?"

Bloody Hand had straightened up, letting his knife drop back into its sheath.

He said sternly, "Herkimer, how many times must I tell

you never to sneak up on me like that? If I had been holding my gun or my bow, you would have been dead before I could see who you were. As it was, I was within a heart-beat of throwing my knife."

"Spooked yuh," the old man repeated, cackling. "Spooked yuh real good." He shuffled around for a clear view of the Reverend Fairfeather. "This one's been on the cactus, ain't he? Then how come I didn't hear him screamin' and hollerin' like all the others?"

"Because he has Apache blood and Apaches do not scream and holler under torture."

"You 'paches," the hermit muttered, shaking his head. "I swear, sometimes I think you're 'most as bad as white men."

The Reverend Fairfeather said in English, "You must be the one they call Herkimer the Hermit."

"You hit it 'most right," the old man replied in halting English, "but you left out the most important part. I'm the one they call Herkimer the Mad Hermit."

While his Indian dialect was fluent, his mother tongue had clearly grown rusty through years of disuse. He cackled at the Reverend, rotating his forefinger beside his temple, then launched into a senseless babble. He broke off abruptly and pointed up at the dollar sign, now fading into the evening shadows.

"Son, I bet you don't know what that there arrow is a-pointin' at up there."

"No, I don't. Do you?"

"You're dang tootin' I do. It's a big cave with one wall made of pure, solid gold—millions of dollars' worth of it. I seen it with my own eyes and I even hacked some out with my knife and brought it down and sold it."

The Reverend Fairfeather cocked a deliberately skeptical eye and drawled, "That's very interesting, my friend, but I'm just a mite puzzled about one thing. How did you go about getting up to that golden cave? I don't see any steps and it's a mite high for a ladder."

"It's a secret, young feller, but I'm going to let you in on it." The old man bent closer and said in a loud stage whisper, "Eggs."

He cocked his head, waiting for the expected reaction. Instead, his listener nodded solemnly.

"Eggs—of course. Now why didn't I think of that?"

"Because you didn't know about it," Herkimer snapped,

clearly nettled at not getting the kind of response he had anticipated. "I kept on eating eggs and eating eggs until I'd et so dang many I sprouted feathers. Then all I had to do was to spread my wings and *fly* up there."

He hooted and shuffled out, cackling to himself.

"Pay no attention to the ravings of that one," Bloody Hand said. "He is as crazy as the horse that has been grazing on the loco weed."

Staring after the bent and ridiculous figure, the Reverend Fairfeather said thoughtfully, "Mmmmm—perhaps! But then, on the other hand. . . ."

Chapter 7

A search of the pockets of the late gold-mining crew yielded a few dollars in coins and small bills but no additional information on the operation itself. The bounty hunter pocketed the money as earned expenses. He rolled the bodies over and removed their gun-belts and guns. The last thing he would do would be to supply the marauding Apaches down below with guns and ammunition.

After prodding the midsection of each corpse to make sure there were no money belts under shirts, he dragged the bodies, two by two, to the canvas-camouflaged mouth of the tunnel. The canyon was, by now, in inky darkness, the Indian cookfires only glowing sparks.

One after another he hauled the bodies out through the canvas and rolled them off the narrow ledge into the blackness. The drop was so great that no sound of their landing reached his ears. That was fine. Let the Apaches go out of their scalps trying to figure out where the dead men came from.

He tied the gun-belts together and carried them up the ladder. At ground level an almost-full moon made the night nearly as light as day. He found a deep-shadowed pocket under one of the nearby rocks and tucked the weapons far in, out of casual sight. He went back then and began to haul up the pokes full of gold dust and nuggets and hide them in the same pocket. It took him more than a dozen trips before the chest was empty.

Afterward, he brought up a couple of blankets and bedded down near the cache and out of sight of the fissure that led to the golden caverns below. Finishing a last *cigarro* before he fell asleep, he grinned into the moonlit night.

Whoever came for another load of gold or to check on the operation was due for a shock. The obvious conclusion would be that the crew had yielded to temptation, helped themselves to the accumulated gold and lit out for parts unknown. In the morning he would help that conclusion along by getting rid of the fancy vests and other personal items that men bent on some well-financed hell-raising would be expected to take with them.

But, in any case, the reaction to the disappearance should stir up a rush of highly interesting and fruitful activity. It might well draw the anonymous master mind of the scheme out into the open.

It was well into the next afternoon when a voice came booming down the entrance fissure. The bounty hunter had finished searching the passages of the cavern and the accumulated stores and private belongings. He froze for a moment, then took a half-dozen quick steps and vanished into a shadowy niche along one wall, gun in hand.

"*Canuse!*" the echoing voice roared. "Goddammit, I've had a long hot ride and I'm not in any goddam mood to play games. Tell those sonsabitchin' knotheads of yours to keep their goddam hands off their goddam guns because I'm comin' down."

After a dragging silence the voice bawled, "This is Red—Red Buckley—and pluck you! I'm on my way down for another load."

Boots clomped on the ladder and Red came into view. He slid the last few yards and whirled around, scowling as he glared about for the men who should have been there to greet him. Muttering to himself, he snatched up the still-lighted lantern and went tramping down the gold-lined tunnel. He passed within a yard of the hidden bounty hunter without glancing in his direction. He got to the canvas screen, swore thickly and turned back. At the chest he paused, flipped up the lid and gaped at it in disbelief.

He let the lid slam and ran, swinging the lantern, into the living quarters passage, bawling, "Canuse, you sonuvabitch, if this is your idea of a joke. . . !"

There was the sound of a wild and breathless cursing. He ran out, stared around, gun in hand, then hurled himself up the ladder, still swearing almost incoherently. The bounty hunter stepped out from his hiding place and holstered his gun. He cocked his head, hearing the scrambling boots reach the top of the ladder and leap off onto the ground level rock.

"Now," he murmured to himself, "the fun is about to begin."

He stepped to the foot of the ladder, then stopped, frowning. Red's first actions had been motivated purely by shock and emotion. If he recovered his wits and began to reason, he might very well come down for a more thorough search of the mine before reporting. The hunter had no desire to be discovered and to have to kill Red Buckley in self-defense. It was far more important to him to have Red rush back to the Spondulix with his report and set the wheels of panic and chaos in motion.

He looked around quickly. There was no hiding place visible that would be safe from a thorough, rationally-guided search. Then his gaze fell on the canvas screen covering the mouth of the gold-lined tunnel. He ran to it and peered out. The entire Dollar Sign Canyon and its north wall were bathed in the glare of midafternoon sunlight.

Far below tiny figures moved, figures so miniature that it was almost impossible to identify them as human. Then from the canyon floor, a figure appearing up here would be no more than a flyspeck against the canyon wall. And the one place least likely to be searched by a frantic Red Buckley would be the narrow ledge across the mouth of the tunnel.

He squirmed out through the canvas, drew his gun again and crabbed sideways, flattening himself against the face of the cliff beside the hidden mouth. With his head bent slightly, he could hear the clump of boots from within if Red decided to return for another search. And, if necessary, he could kill the redhead and wait for someone else from the Spondulix to come investigating and set off the desired confusion.

He looked down to the floor of the canyon. Small specks moved about performing the tasks of an Indian encampment. Apart from these, a tiny huddle of figures seemed to be looking up. But over that immense distance, he could be seen only as a black speck against the gray of rock and canvas.

The Reverend Fairfeather stifled a groan as he worked himself gingerly into his shirt. The Indian salves had performed miracles in soothing the pain in his back and starting the slower process of healing, but recovery was not quite all that miraculous. It would still be a long time before the barbed spines left in his back tissues and muscles had worked themselves out and he would be able to move without pain.

Bloody Hand, the Apache chief, watched him sharply. The obsidian eyes betrayed nothing, but the reek of doubt and suspicion emanated from his squat figure.

"These reward posters you showed me," the bandit chief said, "where will these be posted, and when and how many? If the Chiricahuas are to pay a part of the bounty, these things we must know."

"Of course," the Reverend Fairfeather said, "and it is comforting to know that my blood brother is as sharp as men say he is. More than five hundred of these posters have already been spread from one end of the Territory to the other. You see, I have a great many helpers and informants everywhere and these have been set long since to nail up the posters everywhere. There is no place in the Territory where The Man With No Name can appear today without being a target of bounty hunters."

"It is good," the Apache said, "if it is as you say."

"It is as I say," the Reverend Fairfeather said sharply.

His gear, together with the big Bible that the illiterate Indians had never opened, was piled with the mule's saddle at the edge of the grassy pocket where the animal had been picketed to graze. He untied the lashing, unrolled the fake bedroll and unsnapped the high-powered rifle from its retaining clips. From a pocket sewn into the canvas he got out an oil-impregnated rag and lovingly polished the silver and brasswork of the gun. Bloody Hand watched him with sharp-eyed interest.

"You have a fine weapon," he said, "but it is the hand that directs the weapon and the eye that aims it that wins the fight. I have not yet seen evidence that you are capable of facing that one you yourself said was perhaps the fastest and deadliest gun in all the West."

"Next to myself," the Reverend Fairfeather said.

"Hah! But you do not even wear the small and deadly gun the Anglos carry *here* . . ." he slapped his hip ". . . and with which they kill so many of our people and theirs."

"Perhaps," the Reverend Fairfeather said, "I am armed with weapons you and your people have not yet discovered."

He went back to his saddle, rummaged in the saddle-bags and brought out a slender brass tube with glass at either end and a pair of clamps shaped to fit the barrel of his rifle. He snapped this into place, tightened the thumb screws and threw the gun to his shoulder, squinting through the tube.

"Has my brother ever seen a rifle with a telescope sight that will show him an enemy a mile away and put a bullet right through his heart?"

Bloody Hand snorted scornfully. "The Apache has the eye of the eagle. He has no need for the Anglo's see-far-away stick. Besides, what good would it be if the one you call No-Name is not a mile away but right in front of you with his small gun?"

"Perhaps I can show you," the Reverend said.

He went over and picked up the big Bible. Carrying it under his left arm he walked toward the base of the south wall, scuffing his boots in the sandy soil. After a few paces he bent and picked up a small, flat piece of friable sandstone, half the size of a man's palm. He came back and sat down cross-legged, close to the Apache, the big book on his lap. His rifle leaned against a spiny challo bush, perhaps a yard away. He tossed the fragment of sandstone to the chief.

"Turn away from me, brother, and toss this bit of rock into the air as high as you can. I will show you what would happen to the Nameless One."

Scowling suspiciously, Bloody Hand turned the fragment of rock over and over. Finally he shrugged doubtfully but turned his back and tossed the piece high in the air.

In one incredibly swift, smooth motion the Reverend Fairfeather opened the Bible, snatched out the long-barreled pistol and fired one shot. The hurtling stone vanished in a cloud of flying dust and fragments. By the time Bloody Hand could spin around, the pistol was back in its hiding place, the Bible closed and still on his lap. He smiled blandly at the chief.

"As I told you, brother, perhaps I am armed with weapons your people have not yet discovered."

The Apache took a quick step, snatched the rifle from its leaning place on the challo bush and sniffed the muzzle. His scowl of bewilderment deepened when he could detect no odor of freshly-fired gunpowder. He glared at the seated man, then at the weapon. Finally, he brought the gun to his shoulder and put his eye to the telescope sight. He tilted the weapon up, moving it back and forth in aimless sweeps across the face of the Dollar Sign Canyon's steep north wall.

Suddenly he froze, every muscle rigid. After a long moment he dropped the rifle from his shoulder and whirled on the Reverend Fairfeather.

"It is some kind of a trick," he snarled savagely, "or you are indeed a demon from the black place itself."

"Trick?" the Reverend gasped. "What do you mean—trick? I have done nothing whatever."

"Then explain it," Bloody Hand rasped. "Explain how it is that I can look into the see-far stick and there before me is the one you call No-Name—the one you would have me pay to be killed."

"Wha-a-a-t?"

The Reverend Fairfeather was on his feet, gaping up at the towering cliff. Midway up and a few score yards below the enigmatic dollar sign, an unmistakably human figure stood on a tiny ledge. He whirled and unceremoniously snatched his rifle out of the chief's hands. After a moment's shifting, a poncho clad figure swam into the field of the telescope sight.

"My God!" he murmured. "My good goddlemighty! Mark this down as the day I started believing in miracles."

Without taking his eye from the scope he carefully levered a shell into the chamber of the rifle. The second miracle, he thought, is that at a moment like this my hands could still be steady enough to settle the cross-hairs right on his chest.

From the side of his mouth he muttered, "Get your money ready, brother. This is pay day."

His finger squeezed ever so gently on the trigger. The rifle crashed and bucked against his shoulder, the echoes rolling like thunder between the rock walls and up and down the canyon.

High up on the ledge, the human figure seemed to be hurled violently backward against the rock face of the cliff. But, suddenly, what had appeared to be rock swung open far enough to let the figure fall through, then closed again.

The echoes rolled and thundered and seemed to grow louder until the very floor of the canyon shook.

Chapter 8

Red Buckley spurred his lathered horse down the main street of San Quenada at a dead run. The booming thud of the racing hooves drew several persons to their doors to see who was in such a hurry. One of these was Sheriff Dobrin. He stared at the rider flashing past and scratched his head.

"*Him!*" he muttered. "Now what the hell do you suppose got *his* pants all on fire?" He turned and glared at a new reward poster someone had nailed to the outside wall of his office without his knowledge or permission. The poster offered a $50,000 reward for the very bounty hunter who had visited the sheriff's office only days before. Sheriff Dobrin swore under his breath. "I wish to kee-rice somebody would tell *me* what's goin' on in this goddam crazy county."

He raised a hand to rip the reward poster from the wall, then hesitated and thought better of it. If it remained there, it might eventually bring him some information. He went back in, opened a drawer of his desk and thumbed through a batch of old bounty notices until he came to the one he was seeking.

Whoever had drawn the portrait would never win any art prizes but, coupled with the specific description, it unmistakably identified one Red Buckley as a wanted outlaw with a price of twelve hundred dollars on his sandy head. The sheriff swore under his breath and put the posters back in their drawer.

He was not about to brace the wanted man. For one thing, Red was not known to have committed any illegal acts within the sheriff's bailiwick. For another, as elected sheriff he was forbidden to collect bounties anyhow. Any rewards he might earn went into the county treasury, so why risk his neck needlessly?

Red hauled his panting horse to a tail-down stop at the

unpainted shack that served as railroad station and telegraph office. He flung himself out of the saddle, tossed the reins over the hitch-rail and stormed inside.

The agent and telegraph operator, a long, gaunt, bald-headed man, was at his instrument, reading figures from a sheaf of papers and hammering away at the key. He spun around, wide-eyed, at Red's violent entrance.

"Take it easy, mister. I'll be with you in a few minutes, soon as I finish sending these here car-loadings for the week."

"You're with me right now, pops," Red snarled. "I've got a telegram to send and it's a goddam sight more urgent than your stupid car-loadings."

The agent opened his mouth to assert his omnipotence, saw Red's savage expression and blazing eyes and thought better of the impulse. He got a pencil and pad of forms and swung around.

"Give it to me, then, startin' with who it's to and where."

"It goes to Herbert ..." He paused to dig a folded paper from his shirt pocket and consult it. "... Rebock— that's R-E-B-O-C-K—Mining Engineer, Ferbank Building, El Paso. The message is: 'Hell busting loose. Expert advice needed immediately, in person. Wire immediately when arriving.' Sign it, 'M.'"

"M, who?"

"It's none of your goddam business M who. *He* knows and that's all that matters."

"But I got to have a na ..." The agent looked at Red's deepening color and amended hastily, "All right, all right, mister. I'll get this right off."

"I'll wait right here for the answer," Red said.

"You better go over to the Longhorn instead, mister, and have yourself a few drinks. You hear that there *clackety-clack?*" He waved toward the telegraph sounder that was clattering loudly and impatiently in its wooden half-case. "That there's the main office askin' why the hell I ain't gettin' their car-loadin's in. I got to get them in quick or I'm in trouble."

Red's gun was suddenly in his hand as he snarled, "You're in trouble right now, pops. Either you get my message through and an answer back on the double or you can quit worrying because your troubles on *this* earth'll be over."

"Y-Yes, sir. On the d-double, *sir*. B-But don't shoot me if old man Garrity in El Paso's had a few snorts too many and don't feel up to deliverin' messages till the station stops goin' around."

The bounty hunter stood on the narrow ledge, his ear cocked toward the tunnel beyond the canvas shield, his eyes on the human specks far below. From the sudden scurrying of the flyspeck figures it was rather obvious that he had been spotted. He was not too concerned, however. The distance was far too great for the naked eye of even an Indian to see details, or for their antiquated trade muskets to send a ball. He lounged against the rock, got out one of his *cigarros* and set it to fragrant fire.

A few moments earlier he had heard a faint *pop* that could have been a gunshot, but the range was too great for him to identify it accurately. Probably, he surmised, one of the Indians who spied him had tried an impossible musket shot. They were like children, never able to master fully the intricacies of either the weapons they used or their range.

Suddenly, there was the briefest flash of reflected sunlight from either glass or shining metal. The hunter was familiar with long guns, from the old Hudson's Bay trade musket to the famous Hawken of the Mountain Men, many of which had fallen into the hands of the Indians through capture. None of these had metal work that would reflect sunlight that sharply. Only a modern, custom-made rifle with a profusion of brass or silver, or a brass-bound field glass could produce that brilliance.

There was not time to analyze the thought. The sheer instinct it triggered had him diving back through the screen at the instant the crack of a high-powered rifle reached his ears. He was still falling when he heard the swish of the slug ripping through the canvas just above his head, then ricocheting and screaming away down the tunnel.

Some curious freak of acoustics had the echoes of the shot building up instead of dying away, rising to a muffled thunder. The thunder became an ear-splitting roar and then the world fell in.

The Reverend Fairfeather danced wildly, waving the rifle above his head.

"You saw it," he yelled. "You saw it, you saw it, you saw it! I got him. I killed the bounty killer. You thought my telescope sight was worthless. What do you think now? I've just earned fifty thousand dollars. Get up your share, brother, and get it up *now*."

He had to shout with all his lung-power because the echoes of the rifle-shot were booming back and forth, their intensity increasing rather than diminishing. An Indian howled in wordless terror, pointing up at the north wall of the canyon. The Reverend Fairfeather looked up and his breath locked in his lungs.

The bulging rock overhang that bore the graven image of the dollar sign was moving, trembling, its surface rent with cracks that visibly grew and lengthened. Then with a rending crash the whole tore loose from the cliff and came thundering down its face, breaking up into thousands of separate rock masses. It swept past the ledge where the bounty hunter had been standing, leaving a great pile of rock fragments that buried and sealed off the mouth of the tunnel.

The Indians stood frozen, paralyzed with terror. A great fragment of rock, flying off from the avalanche, slammed down on an Indian, smashing him flat as if he were a bug under a boot-heel. With that the paralysis broke and the entire band fled screeching toward the far end of the canyon, with Bloody Hand leading the race.

The rockfall struck the floor of the canyon with a thunderous crash and a force that shook the ground. Rebounding rock fragments of all sizes flew like cannon balls. Mowing down the stragglers among the fleeing Apaches, the bounding rocks poured across the canyon floor.

The Reverend Fairfeather had been too stunned to move until a slab of rock whistled past his head and awakened him to his own peril. Still clutching his rifle, he scooped up the fake Bible from the ground and ran after the fleeing Apaches with the speed of desperation.

A last great slab of rock crashed down, shattered against the main mass at the base of the cliff and sent a sinister swarm of multi-sized fragments rolling and leaping across the canyon's floor. The Reverend Fairfeather saw the swarm bearing down on him and made a desperate but futile attempt to outrun it. The next moment it was upon him.

A chunk as big as a man's head rolled between his running feet, tripping him. As he plunged forward, other chunks hammered him painfully. He landed face down with a force that drove the breath from his lungs. Rifle and Bible went flying out of his hands.

Half-stunned and struggling to recover his breath, he was only dimly aware of rock fragments pelting his cactus-torn back. Then an enormously heavy mass slammed across his legs, pinning them down, sending a wave of intense agony sweeping over him. He was fighting for the breath to yell from the pain when a flying rock fragment struck the side of his head and his senses dissolved in a shower of multicolored sparks.

He hadn't the faintest idea of how long he had been unconscious. His return to reality was painful and sluggish. At first, he had only a dim and distorted memory of what had happened. His whole body seemed to be a mass of aches and bruises, but the most severe pain was centered in his legs. It was not until he tried to move them to a more comfortable position that the agony brought memory flooding back.

He worked himself up onto his elbows and twisted around to assess the damage. It was not a reassuring sight. A massive rock fragment that must weigh, he estimated, close to two hundred pounds lay across the upper part of his legs, pinning them to the ground. He knew without trying that in his prone position he could never in the world exert sufficient leverage to move it without help.

The frightened Indians who had survived might not return to the canyon for days or weeks, if ever. Old Herkimer the Mad Hermit was nowhere to be seen that morning. According to Bloody Hand, the old recluse frequently disappeared for as long as ten days at a time. Where he had been or how he had subsisted during that time were questions they had never been able to have answered.

If this were one of those disappearances, the Reverend Fairfeather stood a good chance of dying slowly and unpleasantly where he was. With neither his rifle nor his pistol within reach, he could not even take the easy way out. He carried two loaded derringers but they were beyond or under the big rock, clipped inside the tops of his boots.

"Hee-hee-hee!" a cracked voice cackled, somewhere be-

hind him. "Got yourself in a *real* pickle this time, hain't yuh?"

He managed to twist the upper part of his body far enough around to see Herkimer standing a few yards away leaning on his staff, his thicket of whiskers gusting in and out with explosions of insane laughter.

"Herkimer, you can help me."

"They got that poor girl," the recluse said inanely, and giggled. "They think nobody knows where they got her hid, but old crazy Herkimer the Mad Hermit knows."

"Goddammit!" the Reverend Fairfeather yelled. "Can't you get it through your cracked head that I'm trapped and in agony? I need help."

"Heh-heh! You was trapped in agony yesterday on that cactus, but I didn't hear nobody yelling, 'Herkimer, help me!' Now, I've fell off horses onto rocks and I've fell off horses onto cactus and there ain't no slightest similarity. Now, all I want to know is what's so special about this time, except the rock fell on *you?* Are you saying the rock fell off a horse? Or did you fall off the horse *under* the rock?"

The trapped man cursed until he was out of breath, then quieted himself with a fierce effort. Herkimer listened and nodded admiringly.

"You're a real, sure-nuff parson and there ain't no doubt about it. You used ever' word in the Big Book and quite a few it never got around to includin'."

"Herkimer!" the Reverend Fairfeather yelled. "Stop that insane babbling and get that rock off my legs. Go find a long timber or a stout sapling you can use as a lever to pry this rock up long enough for me to drag my legs out from under it."

The old man hooted, slapping his thigh.

"If you think they's any wood like that anywheres in Dollar-Sign Canyon, you're even crazier'n they say I am. Injuns don't use wood except for bows and arrers and fires or maybe to shove up a prisoner's bee-hind to hear him howl. Only most generally for that they prefers a sharpened fence post. Best of all is one that's stood in a fire-ant's nest. You oughta know the biggest wood down here is cat-claw and challo and creosote bush, some of 'em five feet high. You got to climb another three-four thousand feet up to find real trees, and even if old crazy

Herkimer was up to it, he don't have no axe. He don't
even have enough teeth left to gnaw one down."

The Reverend Fairfeather glared through red-veined
eyes. His forehead glistened with a sheen of cold sweat.
He spoke slowly through pain-clenched teeth.

"Herkimer, I need your help. Try to lift the rock just
far enough for me to drag myself out from under it."

"Ain't no use to try, even if I could. A long time
ago—mebbe fifty, seventy-five years ago—I hurt my back
tryin' to lift too much. Hurt it *real* bad. When I couldn't
even lift a whiskey bottle to my mouth, I knowed there
'was nothin' left for me but to come out here and be a
hermit. That's what druv me crazy, dreamin' of the
whiskey I couldn't drink."

The trapped man gritted his teeth and beat the ground
with an impotent fist. He had faced death many times and
in many forms but never before had he been so utterly
helpless. Even impaled on the cactus he had a glib tongue
and a knowledge of the Chiricahua dialect as potential
weapons. Here he was totally at the mercy of a garrulous
old lunatic, who was apparently physically incapable of
aiding him even if persuaded to try.

"All right, Herkimer, but there is one thing you *can* do
for me. Bring or shove my rifle and my Bible over within
reach. The rifle will keep off mountain lions and the Book
will give me solace while I wait for the Apaches to return
and help me."

"*Hee-hee!* You got a long wait, son—a mighty long wait.
'Cause the 'paches ain't *never* comin' back here. Long as
that dollar sign was up there, they figured it was the
devil's mark, tellin' them he was on their side. Now the
sign ain't there no more, they figure he was druv out by
more powerful medicine, so this place ain't safe for them
no more."

The Reverend put his face down on his crossed
forearms until another spasm of pain had passed.

"Then, if you're right, it's more important than ever for
me to have my rifle and the Book. Be a good chap and
just push them close enough for me to reach, Herkimer."
He waited a long moment. "*Herkimer?*"

He twisted around. At first, he could see no sign of the
old hermit. Then, far up the canyon, he glimpsed the bent
figure shuffling along at an amazing pace in the direction
of his cave.

Chapter 9

The bounty hunter hit the cave floor and rolled, hearing the diminishing scream of the high-powered slug as it ricocheted down the tunnel. It seemed to him that the echoes of the shot were growing louder as they ricocheted between the walls of the canyon. He could feel the very rock itself quivering under him.

Suddenly, there was a thunderous rending noise, followed by a grinding roar. The canvas camouflage curtain bulged inward, then ripped to shreds as jagged fragments of rock sliced through into the tunnel. The hunter was on his feet and running as the first chunks cascaded in.

He expected far worse but the intrusion of rocks ended almost as suddenly as it had begun. The grinding roar fell away into the depths and ended in a series of far-off crashes as the rock mass slammed onto the canyon's floor. When all was finally quiet, the bounty hunter took the lighted lantern and ventured back into the tunnel.

The rockfall into the shaft was far less than he had anticipated—not enough to delay seriously the resumption of mining activities. The canvas curtain was in shreds but this was no handicap, since its function had been taken over by a solid screen of rocks that filled the tunnel's mouth from floor to ceiling. At first glance the wall was impregnable, but a few sparklets of sunlight slipping through betrayed the thinness of the rock screen. The mine itself was, in fact, relatively undamaged.

Back in the entrance chamber he blew out the lantern, hung it on a peg beside the ladder and climbed up to ground level. He got his horse and rode a wide down-slope loop around to the entrance to Dollar Sign Canyon.

Leaving his horse back among the concealing rocks, he made his way forward in time to see the last of the panic-stricken Apaches fleeing in the distance. He was reasonably certain that whoever had taken the shot at him was no Indian. In the first place, Indians were notoriously poor shots and whoever had sent that slug was a superb marksman. In the second, it had to have been thrown by a custom-made rifle of extremely high power. In the rare event that an Indian could steal such a weapon, it was highly unlikely he would know how to use it properly.

Gun in hand, the hunter worked his way cautiously through the jaws of the canyon. It was nearing noon, the one time of the day when sunlight reached the floor of the chasm and any moving object could be clearly seen. He paused behind one of the big rocks that framed the entrance pass and carefully studied the floor and lower sides of the canyon.

Almost immediately he spied the weird old figure shuffling along, leaning on a shepherd's crook. He had heard tales of a crazy old hermit whom the Apaches had allowed to occupy a cave in the canyon. This could only be the one they called Herkimer the Mad Hermit. It would be difficult to imagine a less likely suspect for the Mystery Rifleman.

Herkimer halted some distance away and seemed to be staring at the ground and talking to himself. A thin cackle of crazy laughter drifted to the hunter's ears.

A shaft of sunlight was dazzling the hunter's eyes and he took a sidestep to escape it. Only then did he discover the man on the ground, pinned down by the slab of rock across his haunches. A big book and a handsome silver-mounted rifle lay just beyond the trapped man's reach. The hunter nodded grimly. There was little doubt in his mind that this was the mysterious sniper who had tried to kill him.

At that moment the old hermit spun around and went shuffling off up the canyon. The prisoner twisted around to watch him, then turned back and dropped his face onto his crossed arms. His cocked pistol tight against his hip, the bounty hunter stepped from behind the rock and moved forward on silent feet. He was within a dozen paces of the other when he discovered the clerical collar and saw at the same time that the huge book was ostensibly a Bible. He stopped short, his jaw sagging.

Just then the trapped man lifted his head and saw The Man With No Name. His eyes widened and his whole face went slack with shock and disbelief.

"You!" he croaked. "But I thought . . ."

"You thought you'd killed me? Quite a few others have made that same mistake, but never more than once. But tell me something—if that collar means anything, which *is* your principal occupation, killing or preaching?"

"Oh, for God's sake," the trapped man groaned. "Can't you get this mountain off my legs first and discuss theology later?"

"I don't know," the hunter said, squatting down on his haunches. "I haven't made up my mind whether to free you or let you rot here. Somehow, I can't work up any tears of sympathy for people who try to kill me. I guess it will have to depend ..."

"Depend on what?"

"On whether or not I get straight answers to some important questions like—who are you, why did you try to kill me and what's your part in this crazy scheme to mine gold up there and pretend it's from the Spondulix Mine?"

The injured man's eyes went wide for a moment at the mention of gold and the Spondulix, then narrowed to slits.

"I am the Reverend Leemon Fairfeather and that, sir, is all I will say."

The bounty hunter shrugged and climbed to his feet.

"All right, if that's the way you want it. If there's one thing to learn from my trade, it's patience. And it looks as if you'll need plenty of that yourself. Don't go away, Parson Bushwack. I'll try to get back some time tomorrow or next day to ask those questions again. Maybe by that time your tongue will be looser—provided, of course, it hasn't shrivelled up like a slice of frying bacon."

He flapped his hand in casual salute and turned away.

"Wait," the other called hoarsely. "If you really intend to leave me here, at least allow me the comfort of the Word in my helpless agony."

The hunter turned, frowning blankly. "The Word?"

"The Book. My Bible, there on the ground. If you will just push it here within reach it will help sustain me in the ordeal."

"Anything to oblige a friend," the hunter said.

He brought the big volume and dropped it into the Reverend Fairfeather's eager hands, then turned to the custom-made rifle that had lain beside it. He picked it up, whistling softly in admiration, standing with his back to the gun's owner as he turned it over in his hands. He whistled again as he tested the telescope sight on the summit of the cliff. Holding the weapon up to the sunlight, he admired the polished silver butt plates.

Behind him the Reverend Fairfeather opened the fake Bible and took out the long-barreled pistol. He cocked the hammer cautiously, muffling the metallic *click* with his left hand, and took careful aim at the other's poncho-clad back.

"Now that," the bounty hunter said, without looking around, "would be undoubtedly the stupidest move you could make, Parson. Kill me and you're a dead man, yourself. The Apaches won't return for a long time, if ever. The old hermit couldn't lift that rock even if he was sane enough and wanted to help. That leaves guess-who as your only hope of getting out alive. There is only one thing that will save your worthless life—a combination of your tongue and my muscles."

"Damn you," Fairfeather growled hoarsely. He lowered the hammer of the long revolver and slapped it back into its nest. "What have you got—eyes in the back of your head?"

"I don't need them," the hunter said, turning around, the rifle against his hip, "when every move you made was beautifully reflected in these polished silver plates on your rifle. And, incidentally, I think I'll take this along, since it's unlikely you'll have any further use for it. If other matters interfere and I don't get back for several days, I wouldn't expect to find you still alive."

"All right, all right, damn you! I shot at you because you had obviously stumbled on the gold cave I thought was my private secret."

"How interesting," the hunter said. "A gold cave. What is it like?"

Fairfeather closed his eyes, recalling what had seemed to be only insane nonsense babbled by Herkimer, then said, "Mostly it's just a tunnel through the rock, but with one wall of close to solid gold."

"Good work, Parson. You've either been there or you're well coached. Now, jog my memory, will you? Is it the right-hand wall or the left-hand that's full of those thick veins of gold?"

"Why, it's the . . . it's the . . ." the trapped man grimaced as if in pain. His eyes fluttered and closed and his face dropped onto his forearms. From appearances, he had fainted.

The bounty hunter went around the rock slab and stared down thoughtfully at the two booted feet projecting behind the rock. Presently he hunkered down, wrenched off one of the boots and peered into it. He grunted, reached in and pulled out two derringers from small holsters sewn into the boot-tops. The other boot yielded two more. He set them aside, smiled grimly and gave the right big toe a savage twist.

"Owoo!" the trapped man yelled. "What the hell do you think you're doing, you sonuvabitch?"

"Only seeing how bad you were hurt, Parson. Feller I saw once got his back broke by a musket ball when the Indians attacked his cavalry troop. When they saw he was alive, they hauled him off to torture for sport. They built up a big fire and shoved his bare feet in it. He just lay there and watched 'em burn off and sort of smiled because he couldn't feel anything from his waist down. Since *you* can, it's clear you ain't as bad hurt as you might be."

The hunter stood up again, went around to the front and kicked the fake Bible with its hidden weapon far out of possible reach. He moved the rifle a few yards further, as a precaution. Then he went back and gripped the edge of the rock slab with both hands.

"When I lift it up, do you think you can drag-ass out from under all the way? From the look of it, I'm not going to be able to hold it up too long."

"I'll make it," Fairfeather said through gritted teeth.

The hunter squatted, shifted his grip for better purchase and strained upward. The slab of rock tipped up a reluctant seven or eight inches.

"Out," he gasped. "And *fast!"*

Using his elbows for leverage and dragging his limp and useless legs, Fairfeather wormed his way clear in the nick of time. The rock slab crashed down again a scant two inches behind the stockinged feet. The hunter came around and squatted over him.

"Rear up, Parson—up on your elbows as high as you can. You're sporting more hideout guns than a Yankee privateer and I want to be damn sure I've found them all before we go on to the next matter."

"How—how bad am I hurt, No-Name? Are my legs . . . ruined?"

"I wouldn't know yet, Parson," the bounty hunter said cheerfully, "I haven't gotten that far. But just finding out you know who I am is a mark of progress. It opens up possibilities that leave me positively breathless."

Ignoring stifled groans, he peeled off the frock coat and tossed it aside. Then, using his open hands, he explored the injured man's clothing from collar to socks, scowling when he found no more weapons nor any ammunition whatever. He rocked back on his heels.

"No hip-slung six-gun and no cartridge belt, but the best gun in the world isn't worth two hoots without bullets. Naturally, it wouldn't look right for a phony parson to be wearing a gun-belt, so we look further . . ."

Still squatting, he duck-waddled over to the frock coat he had thrown aside and spread it open, muttering, "Ah-ha!"

Sewn into the coat's lining were rows of leather cartridge loops. One row held spare cartridges for the rifle. The second held forty-four caliber bullets for the long-barreled pistol. The last row contained forty-one caliber ammunition for the four derringers, all over-and-under rim-fire guns, commonly referred to as "double derringers."

He stowed the derringers away under the poncho and got to his feet, frowning down at the injured man.

"You were a regular walking arsenal until now, weren't you? Well, I can tell you that you won't be a walking anything for a long, long time to come, Parse. Judging by the way those legs are angled out, they're both broken just above the knees. Now if you'll promise to stay quiet and not get up and go dancing and jumping around, I'll scout around and see if I can find some paloverde branches stout enough to make splints."

Fairfeather twisted his torso far enough to stare up at the bounty hunter with bloodshot eyes.

"Why? A few minutes ago you were all for going off and probably leaving me to die under that rock. Now you get me free and talk about splinting my legs. What made your change? I don't understand."

"Well, Parse, it's like this. With me, curiosity is a powerful itch I can only scratch one way—by getting straight answers. Yesterday I got answers from a fella I figured to be the country's lousiest liar. Today I get some pretty strong competition from somebody else mixed up in the same crazy deal. So I figure being stuck with you for a couple of months might be amusing. Every day I'll ask you a question and every day you'll think up a new lie. So maybe I'll put 'em all together and get the answer by myself. If not, I'll wait until you're strong enough and either beat the truth or shoot it out of you."

"Does it look like—I ever will—walk again?"

"I wouldn't have the faintest idea, Parse. I'm no saw-bones. The only experience I ever had with busted bones was when my favorite horse broke a leg. Ever'body said, 'Shoot her,' but I wouldn't listen. I set the bone straight as could be and splinted the leg tight. Even a real vet said I did a mighty fine job."

"And the leg mended all right?"

"Nope. Couple weeks later I had to shoot her, any-how."

Chapter 10

The bounty hunter rocked back on his heels and surveyed his handiwork with satisfaction. Both of Fairfeather's legs had been set straight and rigidly splinted, the splints tied with strips of fine broadcloth cut from his trouser legs. The injured man was unconscious, having mercifully passed out at the beginning of the operation.

One hand still clutched the bottle of whiskey the hunter had brought from his own saddlebag to serve as a crude anaesthetic. He pried the bottle loose, uncorked it and downed a generous pull before setting it back close to the injured man's hand. When he regained consciousness, Fairfeather would desperately need a few stiff belts to help him cope with the aftermath of the bone-setting.

The hunter got to his feet and paused to light one of his short cigars. He had brought his horse in from among the rocks and ground-haltered him a few yards away. There was little likelihood of the Apaches returning soon and any white man in his right mind would give Dollar Sign Canyon a wide berth.

He studied the unconscious figure, frowning, then grimly shook his head. A strong hunch had sent him riding out to the Spondulix Mine and from then on events had pretty much taken over and guided his actions. So far, however, those actions had produced little more than a spate of corpses and a bundle of very loose ends. Nevertheless the smell of money was strong and growing steadily stronger. Once a whiff of that delectable scent hit his nostrils, nothing could divert him from the chase.

The self-styled "Reverend" Fairfeather gave every indication of remaining unconscious for some time to come. The hunter mounted his horse and set off deeper into the canyon to find the injured man's mule and gear—providing, of course, the animal had survived the rock bombardment. A short way beyond where it had been picketed was the cave occupied by Herkimer the Hermit.

For some obscure reason, the hunter had a feeling that it might pay him to meet the old recluse and listen to his supposedly senseless babblings. Since Herkimer had been living and wandering in this area for yea-many years, he just might have seen or heard something that would tie a couple of those loose ends together.

The hunter came upon the mule first, a handsome animal, grazing apparently unharmed in the grassy area. The saddle and other gear lay on the ground close by. The hunter started to swing down, then decided to visit the hermit's cave first.

The sun was past its zenith and the shadows were already deepening in the bottom of Dollar Sign Canyon. Herkimer's cave loomed up as an irregular ink-blot on the pale yellowish-tan of the sandstone cliff. He dismounted, went to the mouth of the cave and leaned in.

"Knock-knock!" he called. "There's a visitor here. Are you receiving?" He waited and when no answer was forthcoming, he repeated the call in a louder voice, then added, "Is there anybody at home?"

When there was still no reply, he ducked his tall frame under the low rock ceiling and stepped into the hermit's quarters. The cave was little more than a roughly-circular pocket etched out of the base of the sandstone cliff. It smelled like a cavalry barracks at the end of a long, hot foray and was almost as luxuriantly furnished.

At one side two dirty, rumpled blankets thrown across a pile of brush and leaves served as a bed. Near it stood a tin bucket, half-filled with water, with a rusty tin cup hung above it on a spike driven into the soft sandstone. A second spike, higher up the wall, held a grimy rag whose purpose defied imagination. The possibility of Herkimer's washing either his person or any of his paltry possessions bordered on the ludicrous.

A pile of ashes from recent fires in the middle of the floor and a pile of buffalo chips and dry brush appeared to complete the furnishings. Clearly, Herkimer was nowhere around. The bounty hunter was about to leave when once more he was assailed by that overpowering feeling that he was overlooking something important.

He turned back at the cave's mouth and stood scowling at the confined and barren area. Abruptly he went to the pile of fuel and tinder and pawed through it, selecting a thick sheaf of greasewood and its relative, creosote bush. He got out a match and snapped it to flame on a thumbnail. A touch and the makeshift torch flared up, crimson and smoky. He held it high, studying the back walls of the cave.

Almost immediately he saw the narrow black shaft of an opening that had not been visible without the torchlight to throw it into deep contrast. It was at the center rear of the cave and was barely wide enough for him to squeeze through. Beyond it, the cave widened into a negotiable passageway leading back into the heart of the overhanging mesa.

He started in, tripped and almost fell on his face. He discovered his feet were entangled in a pile of fabrics on the stone floor. Squatting down, holding the smoky torch high, he pawed through the pile. As far as he could tell, it seemed to consist of all the multiple garments worn by a lady of society. Never having undressed a lady of society, he was unsure of the names or nature of most of the garments but they had an unmistakably feminine look. Furthermore, in sharp contrast to the stale and sweaty odors of the cave, these were fresh and still exuded the faint, delicate scent of lavender sachet.

He selected an unfamiliar gossamer item, sniffed it and stowed it away under the poncho. He shook his head, muttering, "Why, you sonsabitching old goat!"

The greasewood torch had burned down close enough for his hand to feel the scorching heat. He dropped the remains, tramped them out and squeezed back into the entrance cave. The discovery made him sure of one thing. Either Herkimer was considerably younger than his self-proclaimed one hundred and nineteen years or he was a living example of the Old Testament miracles. Or a lecherous old goat who had somehow recently acquired the material to revive ancient dreams, with no physical strength to activate them.

He remembered a partner he had once traveled with, but briefly. At the time he had been too modest and polite to ask why the partner was widely known as Foot-Sick Feebly. Then, one day, he had stumbled upon the partner out in the brush, fondling a woman's shoe and murmuring, "My honey! My darling! Oh, my sweetheart!"

He had backed away quietly, saddled his horse and

ridden off, to become the lone-wolf bounty hunter. From time to time, as a situation demanded, he had formed temporary alliances, but never again would he accept or fully trust any partner.

Now he briefly considered and discarded the idea of fashioning another torch and exploring the further reaches of the hidden passageway. The day was already waning and the ride to his camp with the injured Fairfeather would be long and slow. He had already been away from the mine longer than he had planned. Sooner or later, someone higher up in the operation than Red Buckley would come to investigate the disappearance of the crew and the gold. His identity and his reactions might well reveal a great deal about the mysterious venture if the bounty hunter were there to observe them.

He started to leave the cave, then stopped, a wicked glint in his eye and a mischievous grin tugging at his thin lips. He got out one of the short cigars, lit it, then walked the circumference of the cave puffing clouds of fragrant smoke. He leaned into the rear passageway and blew a few additional puffs, before going out to mount his horse. Unless living with his unwashed self had totally destroyed Herkimer's sense of smell, the scent of fresh cigar smoke clinging in his private castle ought to drive the old hermit out of what few wits he had left. Here again the reactions might be interesting and perhaps revealing.

He swung wide around the grazing mule and got down, squatting to examine the pseudo-reverend's gear. His attention was instantly caught by the partially unrolled fake bedroll. He let it down the rest of the way, revealing the clips that had held the rifle and the over-and-under shotgun still in place on the canvas lining. He whistled softly, shaking his head in reluctant admiration. Whatever else he might be, the injured Fairfeather was a superbly equipped killing machine.

He unsnapped the shotgun, broke it at the breech and plucked out the two shells. From their heft and the dull rattle of the shells when vigorously shaken, he judged that they were packed with buckshot of the largest caliber. He whistled softly again, but this time not in admiration. At reasonably close range, a blast from one of these could quite literally cut a man's body in two.

He rerolled the blanket and tied the thong, then turned his attention to the saddlebags. One held only personal belongings—a spare shirt and socks, shaving equipment, a scrap of broken mirror and a long, flowing gown-like piece of apparel in fleecy flannel that the hunter finally decided could only be what he had heard called a "night shirt." He snorted and turned his attention to the other saddlebag.

The first item he pulled out was a box of shells for the shotgun, the second a nearly-full bottle of whiskey. The Reverend, it would seem, believed in being loaded in more ways than one. The hunter worked out the cork, helped himself to a generous sample and nodded approvingly. It was a fair enough exchange for the bottle he had left with the injured man.

He heeled the cork back in, set the bottle aside and rummaged deeper into the saddlebag. There was nothing else except a small bundle of folded papers. He brought this out and opened the top sheet. He grunted like a man who has just been slugged in the solar plexus and gaped incredulously at the sheet, a hard muscle jumping along his jawbone.

The sheet was a typical bounty poster, but the image of the wanted outlaw that looked out from it was a detailed drawing of himself, complete with poncho, flat black hat and stubby *cigarro*. Over it a heavy block headline shouted. REWARD—$50,000—REWARD! The text underneath the portrait included even a description of his horse and saddle.

He read it through, with special attention to the list of so-called members of the Organized Outlaws Association. Most of these he knew by reputation and bounty, if not personally. In the course of time, most or all of them would become the objects of his ruthless manhunt. Now someone with a sense of irony had reversed their positions and made him the target, with a price on his head that was as incredible as it would be irresistible.

The other sheets proved to be duplicates of the same reward poster. He stowed one copy away under the poncho and put the remainder back in the saddlebags, along with the other items. There was nothing else of interest. A gunny sack tied to the saddle horn held a small supply of grain for the mule, while a canteen looped over the horn was nearly full of tepid water.

He saddled the mule and pulled up the picket pin before mounting his horse and using the picket rope to lead the mule behind. Fairfeather was conscious but plainly far from comfortable. The level of whiskey in the bottle was a good two inches lower. His deeply-bronzed complexion had a greenish tinge and his face glistened with a sheen of cold perspiration.

He glared up at the bounty hunter through bloodshot eyes and growled in a thick voice, "You took your damn time getting back."

"I had no idea you'd pine for me," the hunter said, swinging out of the saddle. "I was giving you plenty of time to dream up a real good story about why you tried to kill me and who's taking a chest full of pure gold out of that cave up there every week. I expect something original out of you—not an ordinary run-of-the-mill lie."

"All right, damn you! The truth is, I wasn't trying to kill *you*. About a year ago I had a run-in with a hardcase who was drunk and itching for trouble. He'd just found out his wife had been sneaking away regular to see another man and he somehow got the notion *I* was that other man. One thing led to another and he went for his gun, so I had to kill him. His brother, who was even tougher and meaner, swore he'd kill me."

"Keep going," the bounty hunter murmured. "You're doing better than I expected, considering your condition."

"Not wanting any more trouble, I cleared out. But he's been trailing me ever since, waiting his chance to kill me. I saw a figure up on that ledge and took it for granted it was him. It looked like my only hope was to get him before he got me. I got off the one shot and you know what happened then. I guess you'd say it was lucky for both of us I missed."

"That takes a load off my mind," the hunter said, nodding, "knowing the fifty-thousand-dollar bounty had nothing to do with it."

"You sonuvabitch!" Fairfeather said bitterly. "I might have known you'd snoop through my saddlebags. All right, go ahead and shoot me and get it over with. Because I can promise you, the next time I get a shot at you, I won't miss."

"I wouldn't think of it, Parse. At least, not until you run out of interesting lies or I get the truth about the gold mine scheme on my own." He fished the piece of feminine apparel from under the poncho and tossed it over. "Any idea what this doo-hicky is?"

Fairfeather smoothed out the rumpled fabric and his jaw dropped. He twisted around to gape at the hunter.

"So *that's* what kept you so long! Why, you slick old mountin' goat, you! But where in hell did you find a woman in this godforsaken country—and a rich, high-class one at that?"

"*I* didn't—but it kind of looks as if maybe old Herkimer did."

"*Herkimer?* You've got to be crazier than he is."

"I rode up to pay a call on the old loony but there was nobody home, so I took a look around his cave. At the back I stumbled on a hidden passage. Just inside was a whole pile of women's duds, all smelling of some kind of stink-pretty."

Fairfeather sniffed the garment. "Lavender."

"But what in blazes *is* that? I never saw anything like that on a woman."

"You wouldn't, my boy, unless you were married or some place you weren't supposed to be. It's a camisole, more commonly known as a corset cover, and its mostly worn by well-off high society women under their dresses. You say the old goat had a whole pile of these in his cave?"

"Not like that. That was the only one. But there was a fancy dress, a whole passel of short, frilly skirts just alike . . ."

"Petticoats," Fairfeather murmured.

"Then there was a corset and fancy long underwear and long black stockings. Oh, yes. And high button shoes."

Fairfeather whistled softly.

"I'd say that all came off one woman. It's what women pile on themselves nowdays to be fashionable. But how in hell would that old coot get hold of it?"

"Maybe he caught one and stripped her clean down to the buff. Anyhow, right now we've got to get started if we aim to get to my camp before dark."

"*Started?*" Fairfeather cried shrilly. "Now, wait a minute! You know damn well a man with two broken legs can't sit in a saddle to go anywhere."

"You aren't going to *sit,* my friend. You're going to be bellied down, crossways of the saddle, with your legs hanging on one side and your wrists tied to the cinch strap on the other. That's so in case you pass out, you won't fall off and make me have to reset those legs all over again."

Chapter 11

The rider turned his big, iron-gray horse up to the hitchrail in front of the adobe San Quenada court house and dismounted with a flourish. As he tied up to the rail, passersby on the board walk turned for a second look.

He was a strikingly impressive figure who would stand out in any crowd. Standing a good six feet six, he was broad-shouldered and powerfully built, yet there was nothing ponderous in his movements. The youthful fire in his bright blue eyes belied the snowy whiteness of his beautifully-tended whiskers and the silvery locks curling from under his expensive ten-gallon Stetson.

His elegantly tailored suit was impeccable. The pistol slung low at his side had the monogram HKH on either ivory grip. The same monogram appeared on the skirts of his custom-made saddle. A small fortune in gold nuggets was looped across his flowered vest as a watch chain.

He looped the horse's reins over the rail, strode into the court house and opened a door marked: MINING CLAIMS REGISTRATION. A clerk jumped up behind the counter, his smile broadening as he recognized the visitor.

"Good morning, sir. We haven't seen you here for a long time."

"Too many irons in the fire, I'm afraid," the big man said. "I've had to spend more time in Texas lately than I do here in home country. But I suddenly realized if I didn't want to forfeit my gold mining claim I'd better get in here and renew the registration and pay the fee."

"Yes, *sir*." The clerk sprang to a filing cabinet. "Let's see—that name—is—Hocheimer . . . ?"

"Highcomer. H. K. Highcomer."

"Oh, of course," the clerk said, with a rueful smile of apology. "We've had such a rush of filings lately I almost forget my own name. And the location of your claim?"

"South side of Dollar Sign Canyon."

The transaction was swiftly completed, title to the claim ensured for another period. As the big man turned to leave, the clerk said apologetically,

"Excuse me, Mr. Highcomer, but I couldn't help admiring your holster. I've never seen one like it before, open at the bottom with the muzzle of your pistol sticking right through. You must have had it custom made."

"That I did, son. Designed it and selected the skin myself, then had the finest saddler in El Paso make it up for me. I got sick and tired of the common closed holster that collects dust and sand in the bottom when the wind blows and water when it rains. So I designed this to empty itself."

"It's real clever, but with the muzzle sticking through like that, mightn't it catch on the leather sometimes and slow your draw?"

"If it did," Highcomer said, with a touch of grimness, "I wouldn't be here talking to you today. But just to be on the safe side, I filed off the sight. No real gunslinger uses it, anyhow. In a shoot-out, the fellow who stopped to sight before he fired wouldn't live long enough to pull the trigger."

"I guess you're right, Mr. Highcomer. I've only seen one gun fight and that was over so blame quick I didn't have time to see who did what."

"Just hope you don't see the next one over a gun barrel, son. You know what they say—there's never a bronc that couldn't be rode and never a rider who couldn't be throwed."

"Y-Yes, sir," the clerk said, looking thoroughly confused.

Highcomer waved and strode out. At the edge of the board sidewalk he stopped and stood humming softly to himself, running a thumb back and forth through the snowy whiskers. Presently he nodded as if coming to a momentous decision and headed briskly across the street toward the Purple Owl Saloon.

The bartender, a red-faced man with an enormous paunch, greeted him warmly by name and produced a bottle of special whiskey from beneath the bar. He poured, then stood by, holding the bottle protectively and chatting while Highcomer leisurely sipped his way through four drinks.

There were perhaps a dozen other drinkers lining the

bar, several of whom had greeted the newcomer with respectful nods of recognition. A few feet down the bar was a short, very bowlegged man with an ugly, brutish face. His appearance was not enhanced by a nose that had been badly broken some time in the past and apparently reset by a drunken blacksmith.

He had glanced around at Highcomer's arrival, then started to turn back to his drink. Suddenly he caught sight of the nugget watch chain draped across the flowered vest and froze. He turned sideways, hooked his elbow over the bar and stared, openly and avidly, at the string of nuggets.

Highcomer finished his fourth drink and set the glass on the bar with a hand over the top to bar another refill.

"No more now, Dint. This was just to cut the dust and clear the path. I'll be back later for the serious drinking." He threw a gold piece on the bar. "The usual round for the rest of the house and a double for you. See you later."

He nodded to the crowd and went out through the batwing doors. Broken Nose waited only long enough to snatch and down his free drink, then hurried outside.

Highcomer was just leading his gray horse down the street to the livery stable. He paused to tell the stableman how he wanted the animal fed and cared for, then went on to a narrow alley that ran along the side of the stable. He was midway along toward the next street when he thought he heard the soft thud of boots behind him.

He started to turn and a harsh voice rasped, "Freeze in your tracks, mister, and keep your mitt away from that there fancy shootin' arn if you don't want a gutful of lead."

Highcomer turned slowly, holding both hands out from his sides. Broken Nose was coming toward him, his right hand gripping his holstered gun, his left open and extended.

"Were you speaking to me?" Highcomer asked mildly.

"Do you see any goddambody else around here I'd be speakin' to, you dumb fart? Hand over your poke and that string of gold nuggets and be quick about it."

"Sorry, mister," Highcomer said, "but they're my property and I intend to keep them for myself. So you just run along and make faces at someone else who might scare easier."

"You smart sonuvabitch!" Broken Nose squawled and started to drag his gun out.

He had it almost clear of its holster when Highcomer's hand slapped down on the ivory grips of his own fancy weapon. He made no attempt to draw. The custom-made holster was attached to the gun belt by a swivel and the mere weight of his hand tipped it up to the horizontal. The muzzle, protruding through the open bottom, spat flame and thunder. Broken Nose dropped his gun into the dust, executed a kind of slow-motion waltz step and fell heavily on his ugly face.

There was the pound of running feet; a chorus of excited voices and faces peered cautiously from the mouth of the alley. Highcomer folded his arms and waited.

A figure pushed through the gathering crowd, barking, "One side, you people. Clear the way, here. Coming through." Sheriff Dobrin pushed into the alley. "All right, what's going on down here? What hap ... Oh, it's *you*, Mr. Highcomer. What's the trouble?"

"Hello, Ben. No trouble. This stupid bastard tried to rob me of my watch chain and poke. When he pulled his gun, I had no choice but to shoot him."

"Of course not, Mr. Highcomer." The sheriff circled the dead man, scowling. "There's his gun, over there, so it's clear he had it out of leather before he died. That's good enough for the law. You just go along wherever you were going and leave everything to me."

"Thanks, Ben. If you're short of campaign funds at election time this fall, get in touch with me."

He went down the alley, humming softly to himself, shucking out the spent cartridge and replacing it with a live shell. He slapped the gun back into its trick holster and turned toward a closed, unmarked door near the end of the alley. He opened the door and stepped in without knocking.

He was in a small, ornate parlor, crowded with over-stuffed chairs and divans. Heavy red draperies covered the windows, cutting off any light from outside. The room's illumination came from kerosene lamps with red globe shades. Strings of beads covered an inner doorway. Highcomer slammed the outside door loudly and waited, grinning.

A large, buxom woman burst through the beaded curtain. Her hair was a brilliant, unnatural henna, her lips rouged in a violently clashing shade of red. She was still handsome, despite the fact that at close range, the thick layer of rice powder could not hide the lines of age or the wear and tear of her profession. The low neckline of her gown barely confined her opulent bosom.

At the sight of the visitor she squealed and threw herself on him, hugging him vigorously, then standing on tiptoe to kiss him noisily on the cheek.

"Mr. Highcomer, you scoundrel. You haven't been here for so long we were sure you'd forgotten us."

"Why, Marge, honey, you *know* I'd never forget you. I've just got so many irons in the fire right now that I don't get back here as often as I'd like to. I shouldn't spare the time now, but I just said to myself, to hell with it, I'm going to spend the night at Marge's."

"I should be angry with you for scaring us like that, but I'll forgive you this time. Which of your favorites are you going to have—Dotty or Leota?"

"Marge, honey, I'm so horny and so full of spizzerinctum I'm going to take *both* of 'em to bed. But, by God, if they can't cut the mustard, I'll toss 'em out and send for you."

"I'll give them the good news, darling."

As she turned toward the beaded curtain, H. K. Highcomer sped her on her way with a resounding smack on her well-upholstered bottom.

The journey from Dollar Sign Canyon to the heights above, where the bounty hunter had his camp, was a rough one for the Reverend Fairfeather, but it might have been far worse. Mercifully, he was unconscious a good part of the way. Between lapses he cursed the hunter with passionate fervor until he ran out of breath and words.

He lay now on a blanket spread beside the embers of the dying supper fire with his head pillowed on the mule's saddle and his splinted legs jutting stiffly out. His eyes were shut and one hand clutched the neck of the whiskey bottle whose contents were rapidly nearing the halfway mark.

Beyond the fire, the hunter finished scouring an iron fry pan with sand and rinsed it with a dollop of water from the wooden bucket. He set the pan on the embers to dry and stood looking down at the injured man, shaking his head grimly.

"You really slickered yourself good, didn't you, fellow? It's bad enough getting yourself all busted up, but it must be pure hell looking across the fire at fifty thousand dollars you can't collect. You know blame well that even if you figured a way to kill me, you'd never live long enough to cash me in."

Fairfeather opened bloodshot eyes and snarled through set teeth, "Go ahead and have your laughs, damn you. But a couple of months from now it's likely to be a different story. Maybe *I'll* be the one laughing last."

"I doubt it, *amigo*. By the time those legs are set strong enough to hobble around on, I'll have all I want out of you, so there won't be any reason to keep you alive any longer. If a forty-four slug strikes you funny, you can die laughing."

"I'll die shivering if you don't throw some more wood on this fire. In case you hadn't noticed, the sun has gone down and that night breeze is right down from the snow line. It's fine for you because you can move around and stir up your circulation, but all I can do is lie here and shake."

"Thanks for reminding me," the hunter said.

He squatted on his heels, set the frying pan aside and used both hands to scoop sand onto the fire until the last spark was buried. Fairfeather cursed him and tilted the whiskey bottle to his blue lips. The neck clattered against his chattering teeth.

"I'll kill a man," he gasped, "if I figure he needs killing, but I'm damned if I'd ever torture one just for sport."

"Oh, use the knob under your hat for a change. Once it gets dark, the reflection of a fire against these rocks could be seen for miles and I'm not in the mood to entertain callers. I'll go down and get some extra blankets before your icicle dance sets off another rock slide."

Fairfeather raised his head. "Go down? Down *where?*"

"Oh, skip the let's-pretends until tomorrow," the hunter said wearily, "when your wits might be a little sharper. You aren't in your best play-acting form tonight."

Chapter 12

The hunter refilled their tin coffee cups and set the enamel pot back on the fire. He rocked back on his heels, warming his hands around the cup. The morning sun had lifted above the horizon but its warmth had not yet driven back the night's sharp chill.

He nodded toward Fairfeather's steaming cup. "Better put a good, stiff slug of whiskey in that, Parse. You'll want to be bright-eyed and bushy-tailed when school opens this morning."

"School?" Fairfeather stared at him. "What the hell are you talking about?"

"Oh, didn't I tell you? You're attending a now-I-remember-everything class. It's to jog your memory about a few little items like a tunnel with a wall of gold and who's secretly mining it and why. And about a famous mine where the gold vein petered out but they still ship a chestful of gold by Wells Fargo every Wednesday. I know you'll enjoy it, Rev."

"Dammit to hell," Fairfeather said peevishly. "How am I supposed to remember something I never knew? You won't believe it, but the first I ever heard of a gold mine around here was yesterday afternoon when that crazy old hermit babbled something about a tunnel with a wall of gold under the dollar sign. I figured it was just loony chatter until you showed up on that ledge, right where the arrow through the dollar sign pointed."

"You're absolutely right," the hunter said, dead pan.

"*Right?*" Fairfeather gaped at him. "Right about *what?*"

"I won't believe you. Yesterday your story was you mistook me for some fellow who's trying to kill you because his wife ran off with you or with somebody he thought was you." He took a big swallow of coffee. "You see, Rev, that's the trouble with trying to lie when your wits aren't up to it. You get your stories all crossed up and contradict yourself every time your mouth flies open. But if you'll pay real good attention in the now-I-remember class, I think we can straighten you out."

He got down on hands and knees, scrabbled under a rock overhang and brought out two filled pokes. Dropping them beside the injured man he went back to finish his coffee.

Fairfeather studied the pokes in scowling silence, then reached out to pick one up. As he felt the weight of the bag, his jaw dropped and his eyes grew round.

"My God!" he gasped. He undid the thong and poured a small stream of gold fragments into his palm. He wet his lips and muttered again, "My God! Not even dust, but threads and bits right out of the quartz. These pokes must hold a small fortune."

"There's a bigger one," the hunter said, "in the twenty-three other pokes just like them, back there under the rock. In case you were worried about all those pokes down in the chest, you can relax now. They're in good hands."

Fairfeather rolled his eyes heavenward and groaned, "Here we go again."

The hunter drained his coffee cup and got to his feet.

"I'll be down in the tunnel for a bit. There are some things I want to get out of sight before company comes. While I'm gone, you can be thinking up a real good story about all those bags of gold and why they were headed where they were headed until I took a hand in the game."

Fairfeather pounded his fists on the blanket and gritted, "Give me strength. When they put what passes for brains in this character's skull, some poor mule got robbed."

The train from El Paso rolled into the San Quenada station less than an hour late, which set some kind of record. The engine's polished brass glistened blindingly in the afternoon sun. It coasted to a stop with the tender opposite the woodlot, its exhausts blatting, its diamond stack belching smoke and fiery sparks. Two roustabouts, ragged, dirty and unshaven, got up from the shady side of the woodpile, yawning and stretching.

The engineer leaned out of the cab to bellow, "Dammit, come on, come on! Get that wood aboard and fast. We ain't got all day."

One of the roustabouts spat a brown stream and executed an elaborate mocking bow.

"Anything you say, your majesty. I sure hope you remembered to give God his orders for the day before you left El Paso."

Languidly, they began to toss lengths of split cordwood up into the nearly-empty tender. One chunk went wide of its mark and struck the side of the locomotive's cab with a hollow *clang!* The engineer, a small, fiery, red-faced man, exploded from the cab, shaking furious fists in the air.

"Goddammit, watch what you're doing! You put a dent in Baby and I'll put a dent in your skull."

"Aw, don't get your bowels in a uproar," the roustabout said. "If they's a dent, the goddam railroad's got plenty of money. They can get it fixed. It ain't your locomotive."

"Like hell it ain't," the engineer squawled. "This here just happens to *be* my locomotive . . ."

The fireman leaned out of the cab to drawl, "Don't forget *I* got a piece of it, too, Jase."

"*Our* locomotive. So that don't give you no goddam right to bang it up. I—*we*—farm it out to the railroad with our services and anything that happens to it is my—*our*—responsibility. So you see you throw that goddam cottonwood straight."

The roustabout cradled a length of cordwood in his arms and eyed it reflectively.

"You know, Bert," he said to his partner, "if I was to ram this here chunk of wood where I got a powerful urge to ram it, I bet the train wouldn't need no whistle. They could hear him howlin' twenty miles down the track."

The train consisted of three redolent cattle cars and a hybrid half-mail-and-baggage car and half-coach for passengers. The man who lowered himself carefully from the steps at the passenger end was a very tall, very thin, very hipless man, lugging a carpetbag that seemed on the verge of hauling him completely off vertical balance at any moment. Perhaps it was counter-balanced by the heavy forty-five, slung low on the opposite side from a belt that miraculously clung in the general area where most men have a waist.

In the crowd that always gathered to watch the train come in, Sheriff Ben Dobrin started violently and his eyes went wide. He pushed through to the front of the crowd.

"Howdy, Ashton. I ain't seen you for some years."

The thin man swung around and eyed the lawman sourly.

"Oh, hello, Ben." He dropped his voice to a whisper. "Goddammit, how many times do I have to tell you I'm using my right name now—Rebock, Herbert Rebock, Mining Engineer?"

"Dawggone," the sheriff said. "I guess it's because through those years I'd knowed you by so many names I never did figure out which was which."

"Well," the thin man said through clenched teeth, "figure it out now. I've just about had you and your cuteness up to here and out my ears. And by the way, just what do you think you're doing, nosing around here when the train comes in?"

"It's part of my business," the sheriff said. "First I see Red Buckley belting hell-for-leather to the telegraph office and a few hours later here *you* are getting off the train. What am I supposed to figger—we're gonna have a big Valentine party? Or don't you remember it's kind of a part of a lawman's duty to see who goes in and who goes out of his town? So what do you want me to do, Mister Herbert Ashley Middleton Fairfax Pierpont God-knows-who Whatever-the-new-name-is—turn my back and shut my eyes? Did you ever see me lax in my duties?"

"Yes," the thin man said flatly and furiously.

"Oh, *that*," the sheriff said. He gestured airily. "You've got a memory like an elephant, ain't you—and a face to match, pervidin' the elephant is headed north and you're viewin' him from the south. Now, this here train is gonna shunt off those cattle cars and turn around and head back to El Paso. Wouldn't it be real funny if you was to be on it when it headed back?"

"Not for you it wouldn't, you smart sonuvabitch! When I head back for El Paso, I don't plan to leave any loose ends behind to give me trouble. And in case you don't get the picture, *you're* the loosest end I know."

"Dear, dear, dear old friend. Would you excuse me for one moment while I quake and shake in my boots? I'd about guess you were heading out to the good, old Spondulix Mine, old friend. By a strange coincidence, I kind of thought I'd ride out there today too. Why don't we ride out togeth . . ." He stopped short, shaking his head sadly. "Now that's not one bit polite, walkin' out in the middle of a nice, friendly-kind conversation."

The bounty hunter paused at the foot of the ladder to locate and light a lantern, then carried it with him into the sleeping quarters of the former crew. He got the empty cardboard suitcase out from under the bunk, opened it and began filling it with personal items the men would be expected to take if they had stolen the gold and headed off for a big bust.

The fancy vests went in first, followed by spare socks and underwear, a couple of reasonably clean shirts, then the shaving equipment. There seemed to be nothing else of significance. He closed and latched the lid, then scouted around until he found a length of rope that could be looped through the handle so that he could carry the case on his back, leaving his hands free to negotiate the ladder.

He found a coil of light rope, cut off a suitable length and was tying it through the handle when he heard the sounds. They reached his ears as a series of dull, far-off *thuds* that seemed to originate at ground level. It took him a long, frozen moment to realize that what he was hearing were gunshots, muffled by distance and the intervening rock.

He yelped, whipped out his gun, snatched the lantern and ran back to the entrance chamber. From here the sounds became unmistakable gun-shots, coming from somewhere very close to the head of the shaft. Other, fainter thuds were answering gun-shots from some distance away.

As he paused uncertainly, there was a man's high, wordless yell, followed by a mounting crescendo of thumps in the shaft. A pistol came plunging down the shaft, then a man's body, which landed with a bone-splintering crash at the foot of the ladder. A bullet hole where the bridge of his nose had been indicated that he had been dead before the final plunge.

Up above, there were no more sounds of gunfire. The hunter squinted at the dead man's face and muttered instinctively, "Peanuts Posey—five hundred." He stepped over the body and stood at the foot of the ladder, looking up at the circle of blue sky that marked the mouth of the shaft.

The Reverend Fairfeather stared after the bounty hunter's departing back and for a moment he could almost see the sum of fifty thousand dollars printed across the broad poncho in letters of fire. His hands opened and closed convulsively. He could taste the luxurious living such a sum would bring him.

The hunter was squeezing through a narrow passage between two towering masses of rock. With an effort that brought drops of sweat to his forehead and a stifled groan to his lips, the injured man forced himself up to a sitting position. The move enabled him to see through the narrow slot to where the hunter was just rounding a weather-carved sandstone spire.

One moment the hunter was edging around in plain view, the next moment he had vanished as if the earth had swallowed him up. As if the earth had . . .

"That's it," Fairfeather said explosively. "That's the entrance to the gold mine, the tunnel with the wall of pure gold."

He glared down at the two filled pokes at his side and cursed them until he was out of breath. But all the while his hands were fondling and caressing the leather bags as if they were a pair of women's breasts. He was convinced the hunter had left them to torment him with the reminder of his utter helplessness as well as of the twenty-three more filled pokes under the rock. Tears welled up in his eyes and he pounded his fists on the ground in an excess of frustration.

A flicker of movement out of the corner of his eye whipped his attention down past the rock wall of the mesa to the sandy flat below and the worn trail leading down from the Spondulix, far to the north. Three horsemen were jogging down that trail, riding abreast, ahead of the dust cloud of their own making. Where the trail widened and ended at the base of the rock wall they swung down and picketed their horses.

That done, they clambered up the rock wall to the mesa and headed straight for the spot where the hunter had vanished, walking with the assurance of men who knew exactly where they were going. As they walked, each of the trio drew and cocked his pistol as if anticipating trouble.

It was not until they had vanished into the jumble of weird rock forms that realization hit Fairfeather. They were heading straight for the mine and the hunter was below in the mine, unsuspecting and unwarned. If they took him by surprise and killed him, it surely meant his own doom, helpless as he was in his present condition. But even more anguishing, they, not he, would collect the fifty-thousand-dollar bounty.

A mocking ten feet away lay the counterfeit Bible with his long-barreled pistol still inside. A few feet beyond that his rifle, its telescope sight still attached, stood against a rock.

He was already sitting up. He put both hands flat on the ground and levered himself back and around toward the weapons. The few inches of progress dewed his forehead with cold sweat and made him gnaw his lips to hold back a groan. By the time he was close enough to reach the Bible, the ten feet seemed more like ten miles. He looked longingly toward his rifle, but the few extra feet over and back could well cause him to pass out from the pain.

The hunter had emptied the shells from the pistol but had left the spares in their loops on the lining of the frock coat. Fairfeather reloaded swiftly, then inched himself painfully backward until he had a clear view through the slot into the clear space where the mine entrance had to be. He cocked the long weapon and waited grimly.

The trio reappeared with startling suddenness. They were fanned out now, moving on stealthy feet as they closed in on the spot where the hunter had seemed to melt into the ground. Fairfeather laid the long barrel of the gun across his left forearm, took careful aim and fired.

The man in the center threw up his hands, spun halfway around and fell with a heavy finality. The other two whirled and fired wildly, and more or less blindly, in the direction of the shot. Slugs pounded into the softer sandstone or ricochetted with ear-splitting screams from the harder rocks. Fairfeather, however, was shielded by piles of fallen rock. He waited until the return fire slackened, then raised himself up and got off one shot.

The man on the right howled a high, wild yell and staggered backward. One moment he was in plain sight, the next he had vanished into the ground as if the earth had opened to swallow him up. The third man had disappeared completely from the narrow field of vision.

Suddenly he reappeared in the distance, clambering down over the rock wall and racing toward his picketed horse. Fairfeather got off a shot but the range was too great; the slug kicked up dust a dozen yards behind the fugitive.

The bounty hunter's head suddenly appeared above ground. It swiveled back and forth as he peered around, then blossomed into a full figure as he literally exploded out of the shaft. He took one moment to look down toward the trail, then came racing toward the campsite.

"You utterly stupid sonuvabitch!" he spat as he ran past.

He snatched the custom-made rifle from its leaning place against the rock. Down below, the surviving member of the trio was flinging himself into the saddle and yanking his horse savagely back toward the trail, digging in his spurs. The hunter threw the rifle to his shoulder, the telescope sight against his eye. He fired once. The fugitive fell sideways out of the saddle, to lie, an inert pile of rags and shattered flesh, in the dust of the trail. His riderless horse raced off and vanished among the rocks.

"You dumb bastard!" the hunter snarled at the man on the ground. "I go to all the trouble and risk of setting up a trap and you have to get trigger-happy and damn near spring it. For two cents I'd blow your damfool head off now and spare myself any more idiot ball-ups."

"You ungrateful skunk!" Fairfeather yelled furiously. "I go through all hell to drag myself over here to save your worthless skin and this is the thanks I get."

"So who asked you to save my skin? If I figure I need a wet-nurse, I'll pick my own and it won't be one with a face like that monstrosity you wear."

The hunter tipped the rifle over his arm and stamped off in the direction of the last casualty. He turned abruptly and came back, his face an inscrutable mask. He stopped and glared down at the man on the ground.

"Thanks, you bastard!"

"Don't mention it, you prick-head!"

They grinned warily at one another.

Chapter 13

Fairfeather mopped the last dregs of food from his tin plate with a scrap of bread and popped the scrap into his mouth.

"There wouldn't be any more beans in that pot, would there?"

"No more beans," the hunter said, "no more sow-belly, no more flour. When I stocked up in San Quenada the other day I only planned to be out a day or two at most and I sure as hell didn't figure on feeding double. You'll have to hold the fort today while I ride in and stock up."

"All right," Fairfeather said and added wryly, "I didn't figure on going anywhere today anyh ..." He broke off, an expression of wild alarm on his face. "Wait a minute! Wait one little goddam minute! You *can't* go into San Quenada, man. It—it's too dangerous."

"You mean on account of all the punks who'll be trying for that fifty-thousand-dollar bounty, Rev? And if one of 'em should happen to get lucky and earn it, you'd be in a real fix, wouldn't you? I wonder how long it would take a helpless cripple to die of hunger and thirst up here. A week? Two weeks? But don't you worry, Rev. I'm leaving your guns with you. Then if I'm not back in a day or two, you can shoot yourself and get it over with quick and easy."

He brought the long-barreled pistol and the rifle and laid them beside the bucket of fresh water he had brought up from the underground spring. He hunkered down on his heels, his face grimly serious.

"Listen, fella, I want to find out what the hookup is between this mine and the Spondulix. I want to learn what kind of scheme is being worked and who's working it. Now I can ask a corpse a million questions but I can't get a single answer—and I want *answers*. So if anybody comes snooping around the mine while I'm away, use your eyes and keep that goddam itchy trigger finger in your pocket. Is that clear?"

Without waiting for an answer he stood up and tramped off to saddle his horse. He set off northward, following the trail to the Spondulix Mine, keeping a sharp eye out for a dust cloud ahead that would warn of riders heading down from the mine. A couple of miles below it he cut off to the east, making a wide circle that brought him to the ridge overlooking the Spondulix.

Bellied down between rocks on the crest he studied the scene below. The mine property had the same bleak air of abandonment but with one exception. Two saddled horses stood at the hitch rail in front of the mine office. The frightened Mr. Murthy apparently had visitors.

He thought again of the bald-faced lie Murthy had given him—that the Spondulix was using up a rich stock-pile of second-grade ore left over from earlier operations. That it could do this without reactivating the stamp mill to crush the quartz and the refinery to separate the gold from the rock was ridiculous. In its heyday, the Spondulix had employed more than five hundred experienced miners. To claim it was being operated profitably now by a handful of beady-eyed gunhawks was absurd.

The more he thought about it, the more convinced the hunter became that Daniel Murthy's lie had been deliberately outrageous to arouse his suspicions. Coupled with the stark fear in the mine manager's eyes, the tale became an unspoken cry for help.

But what kind of help? And what could be the cause of that unmistakable look of fright in the manager's eyes? Certainly it was not concern for his own physical safety. Daniel Murthy had the bulldog look of a man accustomed to meeting any situation head-on and dominating it. But whatever lay behind this was something too big even for his assured competence. One other thing was interesting and perhaps significant. For a man responsible for so valuable a property, Murthy was the only one not wearing or carrying a gun.

Down below, the door of the mine office opened and Red Buckley came out, followed by a stranger the hunter had never seen before. He was a very tall man, lath-thin, whose gunbelt appeared to cling to his middle in defiance of the law of gravity.

The expensive cut of his suit and a visible air of authority marked him as someone of importance. He might even, the bounty hunter thought, be one of the five owners of the Spondulix. The thin man gestured imperiously and Red almost performed an obeisance before rushing to untie the two horses and lead them off out of sight beyond the idle stamp mill. The stranger stood for some moments looking around, then tramped to the mouth of the mine and vanished inside. Minutes later Red came in sight without the horses and followed him into the mine.

The hunter worked his way backward until he was safely out of sight below the crest of the ridge; then he stood up and went to his horse. Whoever the thin stranger was and whatever was going on down at the mine would never be learned from up on the ridge. But the only way he could hope to get back onto the mine property before dark would be to go in shooting and, as he had indicated to Fairfeather, corpses are usually extremely reluctant to answer questions.

On the other hand, public records, garrulous hotel clerks and cooperative sheriffs could frequently be gold mines of information. He mounted and turned his horse's head in the direction of San Quenada. There was one thing in his favor. The lath-thin man would be easy enough to describe to anyone who might be able to supply his identity.

He had almost forgotten the fabulous bounty on his own head until he encountered one of the posters tacked on the door of an abandoned adobe at the edge of town. He reined in and sat rereading and studying the offer. It had just the aura of legitimacy needed for conviction and the golden promise necessary to win followers.

It was, in short, a deadly time-bomb triggered to blow off in his face or, more accurately, against his back at any time.

Among his peers, Black Jack Oakley had an enviable reputation as one blessed with both superior wits and a streak of incredible luck. In a distinguished career that included four proven ambush killings of unarmed men, three reported rapes, innumerable holdups and robberies and one child molestation case, the estimable Mister Oakley had served just under three years in Territorial Prison. The child case had been nolled when the little boy involved went into hysterics at the sight of his attacker and was unable to make identification positive enough to suit a judge with a well-greased palm.

Consequently, on the rare occasions when Black Jack issued a call for followers to join him in an enterprise, he had to do so with extreme caution for fear of being trampled in their wild rush to respond. This time he used super-caution, sending individual invitations directly to the five outlaws whose talents he judged most essential to the success of his plan.

All were better than average shots, all totally ruthless and all motivated by avarice in everything they did. In addition, they shared a common scorn for the law and lawmen, but a deep-rooted fear of the bounty killer called The Man With No Name.

The five responded to the summons with alacrity. Following instructions, each went to the San Quenada Mission Hotel, asked for Mister Stokely and were directed to a room on the second floor, where Black Jack welcomed each one warmly.

The Mission Hotel was a noted landmark of the Southwest. In the days of the *Conquistadores* it had been a genuine Spanish mission, a great, rambling two-story adobe, built like a fortress, which it had actually been for a time during the Mexican War. The square bell tower surmounting the entrance still bore the scars of *Tejano* artillery fire and the huge bronze bell, cast in Spain, was pitted with the marks of cannonballs. The subsequent owners who converted it into a hotel had left the exterior and its historic scars unchanged. Only the bell rope had been prudently removed after too many well-lubricated patrons of the Mission Saloon below conceived the notion that the town of San Quenada needed awakening at two or three in the morning.

The room in which Black Jack awaited the five probably had the good fathers of yesteryear turning over in their graves. Any prayers muttered there now were made exclusively to the gods of chance.

It had been primarily designed as a spot where a crew of trail hands, headed back from the long drive to Abilene or one of the other railhead shipping points with five or six months' wages in their pockets, could whoop it up in privacy. Bunks around the walls could sleep twelve. A great, round poker table in the center of the room could seat an equal number of players without undue crowding.

Boxes of poker chips and unopened decks of cards were scattered invitingly around.

The reactions of each arrival were remarkably alike. Each man saw the poker table first and licked his lips in anticipation. Then each saw the fifty-thousand-dollar bounty poster on the hunter which Black Jack had tacked on the wall.

Each one flinched visibly and said in so many words, "Oh, no! If this scheme of yours has anything to do with goin' up against Mister Sudden Death, there, you can include me out, Jack. I wouldn't face *him* for fifty *million*."

"Who said anything about facing him?" Black Jack grinned each time. "I wouldn't draw against him for ten times the money myself. There's whiskey and glasses over there on the sideboard. Fill up and make yourselves comfortable while I give you a little lesson in why they call Black Jack Oakley 'The Brain.' "

When they were all seated, he filled his own glass and lifted it.

"To the easiest fifty thousand any of us ever made."

After a momentary hesitation, the five lifted their brimming glasses. A disfigured character known appropriately as One-Ear Gannel lost part of his drink, due to a hand that was suddenly unsteady.

"Go ahead with your spiel, Jack," One-Ear said huskily, "but I got a strong feelin' I ain't goin' to buy it."

"And *I've* got a strong feeling you'll eat those words in a few minutes," Black Jack said, grinning. "You've all seen the bell tower up above us here and most of you probably know what knocked out the big chunks of 'dobe and put the dents in the bell. Mexican artillery fire durin' the *other* war. But I'll bet any amount you want to put up that none of you ever had the brains to wonder why anybody'd waste valuable gunpowder and cannonballs on a church bell and its tower."

A surly man, mockingly nicknamed Smiley Groats, growled, "The damn bell prob'ly woke 'em up ever' morning, bangin' away for early mass, so they was tryin' to kill it."

"Ve-ry fun-ny," Black Jack sneered. He tapped the side of his head with a forefinger. "*I* used the head and found out why. Because Mex sharpshooters posted in the tower were knockin' off the Texans like flies, that's why. And the old muskets the Texans had wouldn't shoot that high up. They had to bring up a field piece finally to clear 'em out."

Gus Shubach, a pudgy man with pale, thinning hair, made an elaborate pretense of stifling a yawn and muttered, "Why didn't somebody tell me I was gonna ride forty miles just to hear what some damn Texans did twenty years ago?"

"You poor feller," Black Jack said. "Your brains must be plumb wore out from settin' on that hard saddle so long. But mebbe it'll rest you to hear who spent part of Monday in the sheriff's office, studying reward posters." He paused for dramatic effect. "No-Name, the bounty killer."

That got to them. They had been slouching in their chairs, looking bored. At the dread name they sat up in unison, like puppets drawn by a single string.

"Mister Sudden Death?" One-Ear blurted. "Here in San Quenada? Damn your hide, Jack, why didn't you warn us? I come ridin' down the main street, big as life, like I owned the town. He coulda picked me off anywhere along the street."

"Relax," Black Jack said. "Right afterward he bought himself some supplies and rode out, headed west. He should be back in town some time tomorrow."

"What gives you that idea?"

"The fact that he only bought enough grub for four days. That means he'll run out tomorrow morning and where else can he go to restock? There's nothin' to the west but mountains and nothin' south but Dollar Sign Canyon, full of Apaches."

"Then, for God's sake," a small man known as Weasel Emory said, instinctively lowering his voice. "Finish your say, Jack, so we can all get out of town before he gets back."

"Hold your water, Weasel. This time we ain't runnin'."

One-Ear clambered to his feet. "Maybe *you* ain't runnin', Jack, but *I* sure as hell am. You never been shot so you don't know what it feels like. I'm carryin' enough lead now to open my own bullet factory and I don't aim to hang around and collect any more—especially *his* lead."

"*Siddown,* goddam yuh!" Black Jack roared, abandoning all pretense of good humor. "Shut your big mouths and listen for a change and maybe nobody'll guess how dumb you are." He strode to an open window and indicated a rope that came down from somewhere above and in the window, terminating in a small dinner bell. "You see this rope? The other end's up in the tower, where one of my boys, Willie Peona, is standin' watch. If he sees the bounty killer ridin' in, here's what happens . . ."

He gave the rope a couple of vigorous tugs. After a moment the rope jerked twice in response. With each jerk the dinner bell clanged loudly.

"So what are we supposed to do then?" Smiley demanded sourly. "Shoot ourselves and save him the trouble?"

"In your case, it might not be such a bad idea and it might save *me* the trouble. Just outside the door, here, you maybe noticed a ladder goin' up through the ceiling. That's the way up into the tower and up there I've stashed Winchester rifles for every man here. I picked Winchesters because they have a dependable range of three hundred and fifty yards. That means they'll hit practically to the edge of town in any direction. You get the picture now, boys?"

"Yeah," One-Ear said. "The bell rings, we all go charging up, grab the Winchesters—and that sonuvabitch in the poncho shoots us right out of the tower. He can blow the ass off a deerfly at three hundred yards—and that's with his eyes shut."

"Not through two feet of baked adobe, he can't—not when cannonballs couldn't even penetrate it. We blow Mister Nobody clean out of his saddle and collect us fifty thousand simoleons. And that's only the beginning. With him out of the way and most of the lawmen bought off or scared off, there ain't no limit to what we can clean up from then on. We'll end up *ownin'* the Territory."

"Or a six-foot hole in it," Smiley amended glumly.

At that moment the rope jerked violently and the signal bell set up an urgent clanging.

"My God!" Black Jack yelled. "He's here a day earlier'n I expected. C'mon, you bastards, before your feet freeze to the floor."

Chapter 14

The self-styled Reverend Leemon Fairfeather bit back a groan as he hauled himself up to a sitting position with his back against the saddle. He glared at his splinted, immobile legs and wondered for the thousandth time if they had been properly set and if he would ever regain their full use. The doubt set off a wild swearing at his total helplessness and dependence. From behind him came a familiar high-pitched giggle.

"Hee-hee-hee! You fit all them words into a sermon, Preach, and I might even take up church-goin' myself."

Fairfeather twisted around. Herkimer the Mad Hermit was leaning on his shepherd's crook a few yards away.

"How the hell did you get up here?"

"Hee-hee! You sure got a poor memory, boy. I told yuh, it's *eggs.* I et and I et and I. . . ."

"Oh, dry up, you big fake!" Fairfeather growled. "You stopped fooling me the other day when I first met you and listened to your cackle. You're no more a candidate for the booby hatch than any of us. At least, not the way you'd have everyone believe. So go shovel your cow pods and buffalo chips in somebody else's yard."

The old man stared at him for a long, silent period. Finally he dropped the shepherd's crook to the ground and stood up straight, looking a good foot taller and years younger. He walked over and squatted on his heels beside the injured man.

"You're a pretty cute sonuvabitch, aren't you? But you aren't so almighty right now, my friend. In fact, you're a pretty miserable piece of gone flesh in your present condition. So I'd say you've got no call to point a finger at anybody else who's got a good thing going for himself. The way I heard it, you ain't such a bad phony yourself. You put on a purty damn good show with old Bloody

102

Hand. I've seed a lot of whites hung up on cactus but you're the first I ever see get off one an' live."

"Let's talk about it later," Fairfeather said, with a realistic groan. "Just let me have the solace of the Good Book for a time and then I'll be able to . . ."

He was dragging the big Bible closer, fingering the lid. Herkimer stood up and slapped a hard foot down on the cover of the book.

"Like I said, you're one cute sonuvabitch. But I got a ace that'll top your king, son—your king meanin' that long-bar'led shootin' arn you got hid inside the book." His hand came out of the folds of the dirty robe, holding a cocked forty-five. "You want to try gettin' that fancy hand-gun out, boy, or would you ruther live a while longer?"

The bounty hunter leaned crossed arms on his saddle horn and studied the poster. He turned his hard, narrowed gaze on the street ahead and saw that practically every door carried a similar rectangle of printed paper. He noted also that although it was only late morning and much too early for a Mexican-type siesta, there was not a person moving on the street, nor was there a horse at any of the hitch-rails.

From somewhere toward the heart of town came the sudden far-off jangling of a bell. The sound seemed to originate in or around the big Mission Hotel, whose battered bell tower dominated the scene. There was a flicker of movement in the shadowy interior of the tower and a long and slender object poked out.

The hunter flung himself sideways out of the saddle as the slender object blossomed a gout of flame and smoke, followed a moment later by the crash of a rifle shot. The slug struck the saddle and screamed away, leaving a pale gash on the dark, butt-polished leather. The hunter landed heavily on his side, rolled and dived into the narrow areaway between twin adobes. His bay horse, no stranger to ambush attacks, lunged after him on his heels.

He snatched his rifle from its saddle boot, levered a shell into the chamber and ran to the corner of the building to peer out. There was a vague movement up in the bell tower and the sound of distant shouting. He threw the rifle to his shoulder, fired and ducked back.

In the bell tower, Black Jack Oakley was yelling, "You

goddam bungler! You dumb, stupid idiot! I told yuh and told yuh—*we* do the shooting."

"And the collectin'," Willie Peona muttered sullenly. "I had fifty thousand dollars right in my sights, and I never had more'n fifty dollars all at once in my whole life. I'd have collected, too, if the bastard hadn't fell off his hor . . ."

Down below there was a flash of fire and the flat smash of a rifle shot. Willie uttered a high, strangled bleat and sagged forward, the side of his head a pulpy mass of blood, bone and brains.

Black Jack caught the falling figure and heaved. The corpse of Willie Peona flew out of the tower and down, to crash on the hotel roof below.

"It was too goddam crowded here, anyhow," he snarled.

Crouched below the adobe side, Smiley Groats was wringing his hands and moaning, "I told yuh so. I *told* yuh so."

Black Jack whirled, swung his sharp-toed boot and kicked the terrified outlaw squarely in man's most sensitive—and treasured—possession. Smiley screamed in a thin, womanish voice, clutched himself with both hands and struggled to stand erect.

As his head lifted above the adobe sidewall, the rifle down below racketed again. Smiley's screams broke off and he fell across the side, hanging half out of the tower. Black Jack, crouching below the sidewall, grabbed the dead man's ankles and shoved him over.

"Now, by God," he said, grinning at the others, "we got us more fightin' room, and one less to split with."

Down below, the bounty hunter jacked another shell into the chamber of his Winchester. Two down, but how many more were in the tower was the burning question. He ran around the back of the adobe and began working his way toward the hotel, using the houses and shops as a cover.

He came to the back door of a place he remembered as a general store, across the street from the hotel and perhaps a hundred yards south. His rifle at the ready, he balanced on one foot and used the other to kick the door open. As it crashed inward the proprietor, a scrawny, bald-headed man, whirled and threw up his hands.

"Don't shoot don't shoot don't shoot!" he squealed. "I've got nothin' to do with their dirty scheme. They

THE DEVIL'S DOLLAR SIGN

wanted me to help but I turned 'em down flat. It don't matter to me what a man does, he's a human bein' and I respect his right to live."

"I can see that," the hunter said.

He shouldered the frightened man aside and reached past him to pull a cocked pistol off the shelf below the counter. He carefully lowered the hammer, then slammed the barrel down on the proprietor's head. The scrawny man grunted tiredly and fell on his face on the puncheon floor.

The hunter ran to the open front door and peered out. He could see vague movement up in the tower. He leveled the rifle and got off two quick shots, then jumped back an instant before a storm of lead smashed into the store front. He ran back down the aisle to snatch two bright new tin cups off a shelf and a new broom from a stack. He threaded the cup handles over the broomstick and crimped them tight. Back at the front door, he adjusted them so the shiny bottom of one cup reflected the bell tower clearly, while the other covered the front door of the hotel.

He went back, satisfied himself that the proprietor was down for a long winter's snooze, then ran back to the front door. The reflections showed no activity at the hotel door. There was vague movement in the tower but no clear target. He crouched just out of the line of fire, watching the reflections.

After a few minutes of inactivity it became apparent that the situation had reached an impasse. The reflection in the cup bottom still showed movement in the tower, but however many were there were staying carefully down behind the shielding adobe. He turned and studied the clutter of assorted merchandise in the store. Suddenly his eyes widened and the ghost of a grin tugged at the corners of his thin lips.

He got to his feet and moved back along the narrow aisle. The scrawny proprietor was making small whimpering sounds and moving his hands as if seeking to reach out and grasp returning consciousness. The hunter rapped the bald head with the butt of his rifle and sounds and movement ceased.

He trotted on to where a wire and plaster mannequin displayed a woman's dress. It took only a moment to snake off the dress. A shelf behind the dry goods counter yielded a bolt of Osnaburgh Sheeting, the fine, tight-loomed canvas preferred as covering for prairie schooners bound for California. Its brownish gray color was not too unlike that of his poncho. A strip of this, slit in the center, draped the mannequin to its non-existent heels. A black Stetson, its crown crushed flat, completed a startling illusion.

As a final touch, he broke off a broom handle, blackened it from a can of stove polish and tied it to the mannequin at the angle a man might carry his rifle. He got a child's coaster wagon from the toy counter, lashed the mannequin onto it and wheeled his creation to the front door.

His makeshift mirrors showed the situation apparently unchanged. He angled the coaster wagon to stay on the board sidewalk for a maximum distance, then sent it out with a hard shove.

As the counterfeit burst out the door, there was a startled yell from the bell tower. Three figures stood up above the wall and three rifles blasted. Three slugs ripped into the disguised mannequin.

The bounty hunter stepped out, his rifle at his shoulder. He got off two shots that sounded almost as one, then stayed his trigger finger because there was no longer a target in sight.

He stood on the wooden sidewalk, his feet planted wide, and waited. The hotel door crashed open and a wild-eyed, disheveled figure charged out, his rifle at his hip. A detached portion of the bounty hunter's mind automatically recorded: "Black Jack Oakley, twenty-five hundred dollars."

"Goddam you!" Black Jack yelled wildly. "Goddam you, goddam you, goddam you! They're dead, all dead—every last one of them. Now you're gonna be dead and I'm gonna be rich. But when you get to hell, you tell that stinkin' bastard Willie Peona I'll be comin' for him soon."

He had the rifle almost to his shoulder when the bounty killer fired from the hip. Black Jack dropped the rifle, spun around and fell heavily, the impact sending up a thick cloud of dust from the street. His arms and legs made a few small, aimless movements, then were still.

The hunter skirted the fallen man with barely a glance. It was not necessary for him to confirm the success of his shot. As the lawyers would say, a bullet hole in the center of the forehead is *prima facie* evidence that a man is as dead as he is ever going to be.

The small hotel lobby was empty. There was no clerk in sight behind the desk but a faint rustling noise came from that general direction. The hunter leaned his rifle against the front, bellied over the counter and reached down behind. He came up clutching the collar of a small, hatchet-faced, pop-eyed picture of abject terror.

The small man's face was the color of a new fine linen sheet. His pale pop-eyes brimmed with tears of fright and his pointed chin trembled uncontrollably. His Adam's apple bobbed convulsively up and down his scrawny throat.

"I wasn't in on it," he squealed. "They come in with guns and threatened me and made me go along with their game."

"You know," the hunter said in a mild, conversational tone, "I've about decided that lying is a lost art. I mean, the real convincing kind of lying. The liars I've been encountering lately couldn't persuade old Noah that it might rain."

Behind him a gruff voice said, "All right, that'll be it. Set Iggy down easy and turn around slow and make dang sure you keep both hands in plain sight every minute."

The hunter let the terrified clerk down, turned and hooked his elbows on the desk. "I was wondering when you'd get around, Sheriff."

Sheriff Ben Dobrin stood just inside the hotel door, his cocked gun in his hand.

"So now you can quit wonderin'. I'm around and you're under arrest."

"You don't say. On what grounds?"

"Discharging a deadly weapon within the town limits of San Quenada and shooting down an unarmed man. I just checked on your victim out there in the street. His rifle was empty and so was his hand gun holster. That leaves you about one step from the hanging rope, son."

"Isn't it too bad? Even if you haul the rope yourself, you can't collect a penny of that fifty thousand. As I read the law, it all goes into the county treasury."

"Don't look so smug about it, boy. On my desk right at this moment is my resignation as sheriff, ready to be handed to hizzoner, our Mayor. I said you were under arrest but I didn't say you were going to jail. In fact, you're going to be kept in a nice, private place until my resignation is accepted. Then I'll start to take you in—just as a private citizen, you understand. But you're so impetuous, son, I'm awfully afraid you'll try to escape and I'll have to shoot you dead. Only as a private citizen, of course. Is that clear, son?"

"Perfectly," the hunter said.

Chapter 15

"Now that," the hermit said as Fairfeather reluctantly withdrew his hand from the big Bible, "is what I call using your head. But like I said, you're one cute sonuvabitch."

He used the foot wearing the Indian moccasin to kick the gun-carrying book well out of reach. He snatched up the rifle and turned it, admiring the workmanship and ornamentation. He brought the telescope sight to his eye and swung the rifle toward various distant objects, clucking softly to himself. Finally he set the gun down, also well out of the injured man's reach, and squatted on his heels.

"Preach, I think it's about time you and I leveled with each other and had us a little heart-to-heart talk. It could just be that a pair of hard-workin' phonies like us might get further as a team than tryin' to go it on our own and likely gettin' in one another's way at every step. Now, I know why *I* been playin' the loony, but I ain't so sure I know all of what *your* game is—beyond the fifty thousand bounty, that is."

"So," Fairfeather said sourly, "you had your turn at pawing through my saddlebags."

"Hee-hee," Herkimer said, mimicking his own high-pitched giggle. "A feller who leaves his propitty around where a crazy man can snoop in it ain't so brainy neither. Bloody Hand and his 'paches snooped in 'em, too, but they can't read so what they found didn't mean nothin'. That's why they never even bothered to open that Bible and see what's really inside, like I did."

"If you can stop patting yourself on the back long enough," Fairfeather growled, "maybe you can tell me some more about this you-scratch-my-back-and-I'll-scratch-yourn deal. I've been in a lot of tight situations in my day, but this is the first time I've ever felt in danger of being *talked* to death."

"You know," Herkimer said, with a natural chuckle, "teamin' up with you could be a real education, Preach. So I'll talk to you a little more, but you won't mind now because it'll explain a few things, like what I'm doing here."

"What you're doing here," Fairfeather said bitterly, "is giving me a pain in the tail worse than one of those old-fashioned highridge saddles. Get on with it."

"Okay, okay. My, but you're an impatient bastard, for a feller that ain't goin' nowhere for a long time. Anyhow, oncet upon a time, as they says, three fellers teamed up to hunt for gold. One of 'em was an old desert rat named Petey, who swore he'd stumbled on a vein of pure gold up here on the mesa above Dollar Sign Canyon. Only he was clean out of grub and half-starved. So he rode into San Quenada for supplies, and when he got back, he couldn't find the vein again. You got to admit these rocks up here look pretty much alike."

"And the excuses those buzzards give all *sound* pretty much alike."

"It's a cinch," Herkimer said sadly, "you weren't brung up on the milk o' human kindness. Howsomever, he convinced two other fellers to throw in with him to hunt for it. One of 'em was a mining engineer, fresh out of college and full of book-learned notions. Th' other was a smart young feller with a burnin' urge to find gold and get rich overnight."

"Give me three guesses. That smart and ambitious youngster was *you*."

"Shucks! There you go, spoilin' my surprise. But you're right about that. It was me, sure 'nuff. And so's you don't spoil your score by makin' a *wrong* guess, Preach, we found the gold vein. Or Petey did, poor cuss."

"Why 'poor cuss'? It turned out to be pyrites—fool's gold?"

"Not on your ding-dang life it didn't. It just turned out to be prob'ly the richest gold mine east of Californey. One day we hear Petey let out a yell, "I've found it! I've found it!" We got there to see him runnin' across a clearing, pointing up at a rock and hollerin', "That's the stone head I told you about. That's right over the shaft.""

"One minute there he is and the next, there ain't hide nor hair of him to be seen. He's gone, just like *that*. We run over and there's a big crack in the ground he'd fell into while he's looking up at the rock. We made a torch of greasewood and I let myself down on a lariat. The crack went down into a big cavern and there at the bottom is Petey, stone dead, his neck broke. I held up the torch to look around and dang near fainted. There's one whole side of a tunnel that's almost solid gold.

"Matt, the mining engineer, come down and he like to've passed out cold himself when he saw it. We was about out of our grub and we needed tools and wood to build a ladder down to the tunnel. So we worked it out that I'd stay and guard our mine while he went in to San Quenada to register the claim and stock up on what we needed. He rode off and that's the last time I ever saw him. I figger he prob'ly got robbed and killed by one of the road agents that was thick around here at the time. He allus dressed like he had a million dollars in his pocket."

"Didn't it ever occur to you," Fairfeather asked, shaking his head in wonder, "that possibly he merely registered the claim in his own name and is waiting to squeeze you out one way or another?"

"Hee-hee," Herkimer squealed in a high falsetto. "Nope —because that smart young feller I mentioned was *too* smart. He figured Matt might try some such trick, so before he left, he went to the court house and registered a claim for a hundred and sixty acres of this here mesa top in his own name—or one fair to middlin' close to his own."

"As one crook to another," Fairfeather said, "congratulations. But for the owner of such a valuable property, you don't exactly live or dress the part."

"If you'll quit interruptin', dammit, I could maybe tell you the rest of the story. When my grub ran out and still no sign of Matt, I thought maybe he was like Petey and couldn't find his way back here. So I built a big fire, usin' green brush. I bet you could see that column of smoke for twenty miles."

"But it didn't bring your partner, Matt?"

"No," Herkimer said grimly. "It brought Bloody Hand and a bunch of his Apaches. They were fixin' to hang me on a cactus when I remembered how a lot of Injuns feel about people who are tetched in the head. So I started talkin' crazy and dancing around the fire and I put it over.

They took me down and fed me and set me up in a cave, and I've been playing the loony ever since."

"It doesn't make sense. Bloody Hand told me you wander off for days at a time. What drags you back to this kind of existence? Why don't you head back to civilized living and start working this fabulous mine? You tell a great story, my friend, but it doesn't quite ring true."

"Because," Herkimer said grimly, "when I went back to the mesa, I couldn't find the mine, either. These torrential thunderstorms we get 'most every day through July and August had washed away the ashes of my fire and all traces of our camp."

"My God!" Fairfeather gasped. "Are you telling me you still haven't found it?"

"Oh, I found it eventually by taking a bearing on the dollar sign. But it was my luck that somebody else had found it first. There was a pack of hard cases camping down there and helpin' themselves to *my* gold, goddurn 'em. Meanest lookin' passel o' gunslingers you'd ever meet. And even meaner looking ones ridin' down from the north somewhere to haul the gold away in saddlebags."

"If your claim is legally registered, all you have to do is report the claim jumping to the sheriff and have him run them off."

"Ben Dobrin? Nobody in his right mind would trust that ranny as far as you could sling a bull by the balls left-handed. If he ever got a smell of my gold, I could kiss my chances goodbye. They say he'd have a FOR SALE sign stitched right on the back of his shirt, if he wasn't ascared of what the voters might think."

"Oh, my God!" Fairfeather said. "And No-Name's gone into town for supplies, with posters all over offering fifty thousand bounty for him, dead or alive. *I'm* dead!"

"Possibly," Herkimer said, "but if you're content to collect that fifty thousand bounty, maybe we can work out a collaboration, like they say in the books. You'd have killed him in a minute for that bounty if you hadn't been dependent on him for your own survival. So if maybe you want to lean on me, I might be able to help you, friend. For half the bounty, that is."

"Keep talking," Fairfeather said through his teeth.

"You stupid or something? It's as simple as ABC. I fade out, and when (or if) that mug in the Mexican nightshirt survives to get back, you kill him the moment he shows.

Then I take him in and collect and we split the bounty. So what's wrong with that?"

"Plenty," Fairfeather said. "You're one real cute bastard, but I wasn't born yesterday. Why should I trust you an inch further than you said you'd trust that sheriff? I kill No-Name and what's to stop you from killing me and grabbing off the whole reward?"

"Not one damn thing," Herkimer said. "For a while I figured you for one stupid little innocent. So now I know you aren't quite that dumb, let's get together and work this out. Naturally, I'd doublecross you in a minute and you'd do the same to me. But if we put our heads together and use them, we can figure out a way to pull it off and protect both our interests."

Sheriff Dobrin nudged The Man With No Name in the back with the muzzle of his forty-five.

"This here," he said, "is the sheriff's office and right behind it is the San Quenada jail, in case you can't read the sign. So get the hell in there and keep them goddam hands up real high and careful moving."

"Whatever you say," the hunter said, "you stalwart limb of the law—even if it's a rotted limb."

"Don't get too cute," the sheriff said. "I might get caught up in a rash of integrity." He threw his gun on the littered desk and added the handcuffs from his belt. "You maybe noted, I didn't take your gun from under the fancy rug you wear. So grab them cuffs and cuff me to, say, the leg of the desk, so's I can push myself off and start yelling for help right after you make your big break."

The bounty hunter stared at him.

"I only know two languages, English and profane, and you don't make much sense in either one."

"I expect not," the sheriff said. "But if you had to try to hang onto your office in a town overrun with outlaws and give honest folk a fair amount of protection, you'd play games, too. So never mind the big arguments. Handcuff me to a leg of the desk, grab my gun along with your own and get the hell on your way. How much time do you need before I start yelling?"

"Time enough to buy groceries and check on a mining claim registration at the court house."

"You've got a half-hour, buster. Then I start yelling and when I yell, mister, there ain't nobody in this county goin' to stay asleep. So you'd better do whatever you have to do and be well on your way when I cut loose. And by the way, you'd better tell me which way you're headed, so's if I get up a posse I can be sure to lead 'em in the wrong direction."

"Why," the hunter said blandly, "I hear tell the badlands over west of the Spondulix Mine make great hideout country for outlaws. That means it ought to be a great hunting ground for my kind of business. All of which reminds me, I left some pretty valuable merchandise strewn around the bell tower and roof of the Mission Hotel. As I recall, the total bounty came to something like seventy-six hundred dollars."

"You *would* recall that, right down to the penny," the sheriff said. He squatted in front of the safe and spun the dial. "I've heard about a machine that adds up money, but this is the first time I ever seen one that walked around on two legs."

Chapter 16

Belly down on the flat top of a weather sculptured sandstone spire, Herkimer made a final sweep of the horizon with his spy glass, pausing at intervals to study objects of particular interest. At last he closed the glass with a snap and inched himself back to the edge of the natural platform. Finding precarious hand- and footholds in the crumbling sandstone, he eased himself down and tramped back to where the pseudo-Reverend Fairfeather lay with his head on the mule saddle.

"He's comin'. About two mile off yet, I judge."

"You're dead certain it's The Man With No Name?"

"Now, what the hell kind of idiotic question is that?" Herkimer demanded testily. "You know anybody else who runs around in a crazy get-up like that?"

"Yes," Fairfeather said sardonically. "A nut who calls himself Herkimer the Mad Hermit. But that's beside the point right now. If I'm to go through with your big scheme, you'd getter give me back my pistol."

"My big scheme is *kaput,* as the Dutchies say, for the time being, anyhow. He ain't the only one headed this way. We got company coming from dang near every point o' the compass. When they meet, this place is goin' to look like either a convention or a slaughterhouse."

Fairfeather hauled himself up onto his elbows, stifling a groan. "What do you mean?"

"My God, I never knowed anybody who could ask so many damfool questions as you. What the hell do you think I mean when I say there's others heading this way? In the fust place there's somebody trailin' your No-Name feller, keepin' well behind and ridin' easy so's not to kick up too much dust. Then there's five or six riders in a bunch comin' down that trail from the north, an' they're really shovelin' on the coal. You don't need a glass to see their dust cloud from ten miles off."

115

"Then No-Name has spotted it and will take whatever precautions necessary to protect himself."

Herkimer snorted. "I've seen some funny set-ups in my day, but this here takes the cake. You're worryin' about his safety and at the same time, plottin' to kill him yourself."

"Naturally," Fairfeather snapped. "How could I kill him and collect the fifty thousand if he's already dead?"

"*We* collect the fifty thousand, son. And just so's you don't get forgetful about it, when I do hand you back your gun, it'll have just *one* bullet in it. Now, that gives you a real tough choice. You can either use that bullet to kill No-Name the moment his back is turned, or you can use it to kill me. Either way's a big gamble for you. If you kill him, you don't know but what I'll kill you and claim the whole bounty. On the other hand, if you kill me, you might never get another chance at him. Puts you in kind of a swivet, don't it?"

Fairfeather cursed him until he was out of breath. He sank back onto the saddle, his face gray with pain.

"Someone following No-Name and maybe six riders coming down the trail doesn't sound like the big convention you made it out to be."

"You got smart and didn't let me finish. Headin' this way from over toward the badlands country is a freight wagon with maybe a dozen or more riders bunched around it. An' over east, mighty nigh to the horizon, there's the biggest goldurn dust cloud you ever seed, like the whole Yew-nited States cavalry was headin' here at a dead gallop. When they all meet, guess who's goin' to be right spang in the middle."

"We are."

"Wrong, boy. *You* are—because I got more important things to do than hang around here gettin' shot at. Of course, if you want to get up and run away, too, go right ahead."

"The worst thing about being crippled like this is having to lie here and listen to that tired old joke over and over and over again. But before you skedaddle, Herk, old boy, tell me one thing. Now that you're too old to rightly enjoy a woman, do you get your pleasure out of keeping a pile of their underwear around to fondle and play with?"

"Who the hell says I'm too old to rightly enjoy a woman?" Herkimer bellowed furiously. "By God, I'm a better man . . ." He broke off, his face suffused with rage. "So *that's* who come sneakin' around my cave, stinkin' it up with his goddam cigar smoke. Well, let me tell you, you bastard, what I got there and what I do with it is none of your goddam business, nor his, neither, the sonuvabitch."

Muttering, "Too old, goddam 'im," he tramped to where he had dropped Fairfeather's pistol and rifle. He brought them over and laid them down just beyond their owner's reach. Breaking a branch off a stunted challo bush, he came back and tossed it on Fairfeather's chest.

"I don't know why I should do you any favors, damn your hide, but I guess I wasn't born as gut mean as some people I could spit on from here. I purely hate to see a man lie helpless with nothin' to do to occupy his time. You use this here twig real careful, so's it don't break, and you can have yourself an hour or more of fun draggin' your guns close enough to grab. Meantime, I'll wish you luck—which you're goin' to need plenty of—and be on my way. *Adios, maleante,* and in case your education's been neglected, that's Mex for goodbye, you dirty crook."

He snatched up his shepherd's staff and scuttled off, to vanish in the forest of rock spires. Fairfeather swore thickly and twisted his upper body as far as he could in a futile effort to reach his weapons. Despite a struggle that brought a sheen of sweat to his forehead, they remained a tantalizing six or seven inches beyond his fingertips. It took him the better part of an hour to work them within reach, using the frail and tormentingly flexible challo twig.

At the edge of the rock-strewn flat below the edge of the mesa, the bounty hunter dismounted and studied the head-high growth of ground cover. A spreading paloverde caught his eye. Using the tight-woven poncho to shield his hands, he worked it loose from the sandy ground, then used his sheath knife to cut the tap root that would plunge for yards into the depths in its search for the water level.

He noosed the shrub to the end of his lariat, secured the other end to his saddle horn and remounted. Riding on, he looked back and nodded with satisfaction. The spreading paloverde successfully smoothed out the sand, wiping out all traces of hoof prints. It did raise a thick cloud of dust, which could not be helped, but the last time he looked, his tracker had been too far back to make use of the betraying sign and in among the rocks it would swiftly dissipate.

A devious route brought him to an open glade where there was good grazing as well as shade. He stripped and picketed his horse, then finally climbed to a rock spire that gave him a good view of his back trail. His trailer was still there, now almost to the edge of the rock field and drifting cautiously from cover to cover.

He briefly considered going down for his spy glass, then shrugged off the notion. After all, he had a fairly good idea who was following him and why, and his theory opened a wide field of possibilities toward solving the whole mystery of the mines.

Northward, the riders pounding down from the direction of the Spondulix were less than two miles away. To the west, the group escorting the freight wagon were still some miles off. Whoever was raising the enormous dust cloud in the east could not possibly arrive until late in the day so they could be counted out as an immediate factor.

He scrambled down and untied the two gunny sacks from his saddle horn. One held their food supplies and the other grain for the horse and mule. Hoisting them over his shoulders, he clambered up the rock wall and made his way to the spot where Fairfeather lay. He stopped a few yards away and wrinkled his nose.

"Phew! What was *he* doing up here?"

"What was *who* doing?"

"You know damn well *who*. Either Herkimer was here or you have been entertaining a herd of goats and in your present condition you aren't exactly up to that."

"All right," Fairfeather acknowledged sullenly. "He was here. How that crazy old coot gets around this far, I'll never know, but here he came, shuffling and giggling and talking his crazy nonsense."

"Like how about you two should team up to kill me for the bounty, maybe?"

Fairfeather glared at him. "You're too goddam smart for your own good."

"So I've been told," the bounty hunter said mildly, easing the sacks of provisions to the ground and leaning his rifle against the rock overhang. "But being smart can lead to some interesting discoveries. For instance, do you know who owns the mine with the wall of gold over there, by virtue of registering the claim and paying the fee regularly—like only yesterday?"

"How would I know?"

"I thought maybe he'd told you. The claim is registered in the name of H. K. Highcomer, which is probably phony—the H standing for Herkimer who, as you've no doubt already discovered, is crazy like a fox."

"Why tell me?" Fairfeather yelled furiously. "Even if I gave a damn, what could I do about it?"

"Sweat and stew," the hunter said affably. "Right over there, almost at your fingertips, is a mine worth maybe two-three million dollars. To say nothing of a body worth fifty thousand right here. Anybody as money-hungry as you is first going to just about drive himself nuts over it. Then he's going to get hold of himself and start plotting and scheming. Sooner or later I'm betting you'll cook up some harebrained trick that I can grab off for myself. It's so much easier to let someone else do the brain work."

He picked up the custom-built rifle with the telescope sight and leaned it against the rock beside his own.

"Hey, hey, hey!" Fairfeather yelled indignantly. "What the hell do you think you're doing with my rifle, you bastard? I didn't give you per. . . ."

"Just borrowing it, my friend, to protect you from what the newspapers call tragic consequences. Flat on your back, you couldn't hit the side of a barn unless it was flying overhead. You'd probably end up by shooting off your own toes." He got down on his knees and fished the hollowed-out Bible from under the overhanging rock. Dropping it beside the injured man, he said, "I'd suggest you put that junior size cannon back inside the book and keep it out of sight unless you absolutely *have* to use it."

Fairfeather rolled his eyes up and demanded plaintively, "Will sombeody pleeease tell me what the hell is going on or about to? Here I am, practically a helpless cripple, and this idiot is playing games like a man getting ready for another war."

"Maybe I am," the hunter said, suddenly grim. "We're sitting here in what sailors call the eye of the hurricane. We've already got one uninvited visitor who trailed me out from San Quenada and is prowling around here somewhere. Then there's one bunch of riders pounding hell-for-leather down the trail from the Spondulix Mine and another bunch heading this way from the badlands to the west. If that isn't enough possible trouble, there's the damndest biggest dust cloud you ever saw rolling this way from the east and I'm damn sure it isn't being kicked up by jack rabbits. I'm just as sure they're not heading here for a big barbecue and political rally. When they all come together, all hell is liable to bust loose, with us caught right in the middle. So keep your shooting iron handy and your cards close to your vest, brother."

"Thanks for letting me in on your secrets. If I'm going to be killed, I always think it's kind of nice to know who by and what for."

"I'll try to get you the answers to both questions," the bounty hunter said. He cradled his rifle in the crook of his left arm. "While I scout around a bit, you can lie there and stew yourself into a lather over how you're going to sell out to the highest bidder before the shooting starts."

From directly behind him a harsh voice rasped, "Correction, Mister Nobody from Nowhere. You ain't goin' any place except where I tell you and when I tell you."

Without looking around the hunter said affably, "Well howdy, sheriff. I was wondering how long it would take you to pick up my trail again and follow it here. It's plain to see that tracking isn't one of your strong points. Coming out from San Q you'd have lost me a couple of times if I hadn't held back to let you catch up again and made sure to keep to soft ground where my tracks would be easy to see and follow."

Sheriff Ben Dobrin stood a few yards behind him, feet planted wide apart, his cocked gun steady against his hip. His face was dark and ugly.

"You're so goddam smart, then you're smart enough to know how painful it can get if you don't speak up and answer right out. *Where is it?*"

"It?" the hunter asked innocently. "Do I have something of yours, sheriff?"

"You know goddam well you have," the sheriff said in a choked and furious voice. "A whole week's output of gold, is all. Close to seventy thousand dollars' worth and not ore but pure bullion. *Where—is—it?*"

"Oh, bless my soul," the hunter said. He started to turn, scratching his head. "Now, where could I have put that. . . ?"

"Hold it!" the sheriff barked. "First, you drop that rifle. Then you do the same with the hand gun under that poncho and *then* you can swing around and start talking." He added through clenched teeth, "You even *think* about

tryin' one funny move and you get it right through the
back."

"That's using the old head," the hunter said. He leaned
his rifle against the rock, then dropped his forty-four to
the ground beside it. "If I'm dead, you can question me
for hours without the slightest danger of my giving you
trouble. On the other hand, old chap, you can question my
corpse for hours without my giving you the answer you
want, either. So where does that leave us, do you suppose?"

"I'll tell you where it leaves *me*," Fairfeather broke in
shrilly. "It leaves me in the driver's seat. Because I happen
to know where those twenty-odd pokes of raw gold are
and I'm a reasonable man, willing to bargain."

"Bargain?" the sheriff's head snapped around. "Bargain
for what?"

"My life and, of course, a reasonable share of the gold.
You'll find me remarkably easy to do business with, sheriff.
I am not a greedy man."

"If this is a scheme to help your friend ..."

"*Friend?*" Fairfeather squawled. "I was trying to kill
him for the bounty when my plan backfired and left me
crippled like this. Don't call him my friend."

"Oh, sure. So he brung you here and splinted your legs
and is nursemaidin' you just out of the goodness of his
heart. I know exactly how those things go."

"Dammit to hell!" Fairfeather yelled. "He brung—
brought me here because he thinks I know where a treasure is hidden and he planned to beat it out of me while
I'm too helpless to protect myself. I've told him and told
him there isn't any such treasure, but he's the kind of
two-legged jackass gets a damfool idea in his head and
you can't shake him loose from it."

"Crooks I can understand," the sheriff said. "It's only
so-called honest men that mix me up. Ten per cent of the
gold and I take care of you until you're up and around
again."

"*Twenty* per cent. After all ..."

"Twenty it is, then. I can be a reasonable man, too."

The bounty hunter had folded his arms and leaned
against the overhanging rock, following the conversation
with bright-eyed interest. He clucked sadly and shook his
head.

"I'm afraid I misjudged you, Preach. Here, all the time

I had you figured for a smart man, but you're the worst
kind of fool. Even kids swapping marbles have sense
enough not to grab the first offer. They get three-four
others and play them off, one against the other, until they
know for sure they're getting the absolute top deal. You
grab the first one that comes along and you'll likely get
skinned out of that. I've got a feeling our sheriff, here,
isn't completely honest."

Dobrin whirled on him, his face black with fury. "Shut
up, goddam you! *Shut up!* If the gold is where he says it
is, *you're* a dead man—and if it ain't, *he's* dead!" He
gestured sharply with the gun. "Get away from your guns,
damn yuh! ! Get the hell far away and then stay put." The
bounty hunter obediently moved yards away from the
weapons he had dropped.

He clasped hands at the back of his neck and looked
bored.

"I do hope you'll forgive me for looking bored, but I've
been threatened by so many cheap crooks in my lifetime
that I simply can't muster up an expression of alarm.
However, if things get really rough and I seem to be in
danger, I just might sweat a little. It depends pretty much
on how well the Rev, here, comes through with his big
promise to sell me out."

"Damn you," Fairfeather panted, "I'll come through,
never you fret. Maybe you forget that you showed me two
of the pokes and told me where twenty-odd more were
stashed. You even put the two back right while I was
watching. So there you are, sheriff. Your gold—*our* gold—
is right under that big rock overhang over there. You'll
have to scrootch down quite a bit, because it's way back,
against the back side, but it's there."

"It goddam better be," the sheriff growled. "For your
sake as well as his, damn yuh."

The bounty hunter blew on his fingernails and polished
them vigorously on his shirt sleeve. His expression revealed the excitement and interest of a man bound for a
Sabbath meeting.

Still covering the hunter and watching him sharply, the
sheriff dropped down on his heels and threw a sharp look
back into the shadowy space back under the rock. He
looked back at the hunter, then under the rock again, then
back. He worked backward on his heels and risked another quick look.

He stood up, his face suffused with rage, his breath coming in tight, shallow gasps. Without a word he straightened up, walked to the injured man's bed. Panting, he kicked Fairfeather in the face, opening a bloody gash on the side of his cheek.

"You cute sónuvabitch! You smart almighty bastard! If you figured on giving your partner his chance to make a play then by God, you guessed wrong. I ain't fallin' for that crap from nobody, goddam yuh!"

"You mean the pokes of gold aren't there?" the bounty hunter said. "Oh, my goodness! Do you suppose I could have absentmindedly misplaced them somewhere?"

Chapter 17

The hunter whirled on Fairfeather, who was holding a bloody handkerchief to his gashed cheek and looking utterly dumbfounded.

"You did it, you rat! *You're* the one who moved the gold to a new hiding place while I was in town for supplies. You're the only one who knew where it was because I showed you, and I even handed you two pokes to open and see for yourself how rich it was."

"You're out of your mind," Fairfeather screeched wildly. "You're even crazier than that crazy Herkimer. How could I even look for a new hiding place, let alone move all the gold to it, with two broken legs? Here I am, a helpless cripple, and you accuse me of robbing you. You're trying to shove the blame on me and get me killed."

"Yeah, fellow," Sheriff Dobrin panted, his eyes glittering with rage. "If you expect to sell me that yarn, you'd better do some fast explaining."

"How would I know if his legs are really broken, sheriff?" the hunter demanded. "I'm no doctor. He said they were broken and begged me to put splints on them, so I just did the way I'd seen the sawbones do hundreds of times in the Army."

"By God," the sheriff roared. He snatched up the hunter's rifle, holding it by the muzzle, and advanced on Fairfeather, his face a mask of savagery. "They better, by God, be broke or I'll break them, inch by inch, from your crotch to your toes, damn yuh, if you don't spit out the truth."

"Shh! Shh!" the hunter said, finger to his lips. "Keep it low, sheriff, if you don't want *them* to hear you."

"Them?" the sheriff husked in a slightly modified bellow. "What do you mean—*them?* If this is another of your tricks . . ."

124

"Look for yourself," the hunter said, jerking his head toward the edge of the mesa. "They just rode in from the north and are picketing their horses down there below the wall. From the way they're lathered up, they must have been really pushing those horses."

The sheriff peered around the rock and cursed wildly. "Those nervy sonsabitches!" He snatched up Fairfeather's rifle and the hunter's pistol. "I'll be right back and you'd better, by jeez, be here, fella, or God help you when I run you down."

He galloped toward the rim of the mesa bellowing, "That's far enough! Hold it right there, you buzzards!"

"You bastard!" Fairfeather said bitterly. "Trying to dump your thievery on a helpless cripple."

"Use your head, you idiot," the hunter snapped. "How else could I keep him from killing you on the spot? He'll probably give you some of the treatment you richly deserve, but he'll keep you alive as long as he thinks there's a chance you know where the gold really is hidden."

He bent, snatched the long-barreled pistol from its hiding place in the fake Bible and raced off, followed by Fairfeather's yell of anguished outrage.

The custom-made weapon was much too long to fit into his holster. He tucked it into the waistband of his trousers as he darted from rock cover to rock cover. Long before he came to the edge of the mesa he could hear voices raised in angry altercation. His eyes glittered with anticipation. There was nothing like a furious blow-up to spill closely-guarded secrets.

At the edge of the mesa he peered cautiously around the shielding rock. Sheriff Dobrin and the new arrivals were almost directly below. The sheriff had the rifles tucked under his left arm. His right hand was holding his cocked pistol, the muzzle almost poking the belly of the slat-thin man who had appeared to wield so much authority at the Spondulix Mine.

Standing back, hands close to their holstered guns, were Red Buckley and two other typical gunslinger types. A fifth man, standing a little apart, was Dan Murthy, superintendent of the Spondulix. Once again the hunter noted that Murthy was the only one not wearing a gun. The fact was beginning to take on a new significance in his mind.

"You dirty, stinkin', no-good, doublecrossing skunk,"

the sheriff was yelling. "Roebuck, or Ashley or Middleton or whatever the goddam hell your phony name is right now, I wish to hell I'd put the cuffs on you the minute I seen you step off that train. And don't think I ain't got enough on you to keep you in Territorial prison the rest of your goddam life."

"With guess-who as my next-door cellmate," the thin man said sarcastically. "You try to turn me in, you stupid bastard, and I'll see you get the tighest security cell they ever built. What I could tell would win you the biggest double hanging in years."

"Not without solid evidence," Sheriff Dobrin shouted, "and I had sense enough to cover my tracks all the way—which is a goddam sight more sense than you had. You go ahead and make any charges you want, but just try to prove even one of 'em, you conniver."

"You aren't even a half-smart crook," the thin man sneered. "You're a cheap-john alleybagger trying to move up out of your class."

"Yeah? Who thought up the whole scheme, you sonuvabitch? Whose idea was this?"

"Yours," the thin man said wearily. "And a dumber, cruder plan I never heard. It would have earned you a hanging in the first week if I hadn't added the refinements that made it a work of genius. That's why I cut you out. I'm sick and tired of pouring profits down that rat hole you use for a brain while I still have to handle every emergency that comes up."

"Like you handled this one," the sheriff yelled, "you braggin' sonuvabitch! Do *you* know what became of the mine crew that disappeared? Do *you* know who got away with a week's output in pure gold? Do *you* know where the thief is right now? You're goddam right you don't, you smart bastard. But *I* know the answer to every one of those questions and before sundown today I'll have that gold back in my hands, every ounce of it. So tell me again how much smarter you are than I am, you penny ante genius."

The two were almost nose-to-nose, shouting furiously at one another in a mounting crescendo of unbridled fury. The gun was shaking violently in the sheriff's hand. The thin man leaned forward stiffly, as if only invisible wires restrained him from going for his own weapon. The three gunslingers had unobtrusively fanned out, clawed hands hovering over gun butts. The very atmosphere seemed to crackle with the rising tension. The explosion was a matter of moments away.

The bounty hunter eased the long pistol out of his waistband and cocked it, ready to jump in shooting to take control of the situation however it developed. He set himself to move, then froze.

Less than a hundred yards away, a weird and ghostlike figure was drifting among the rocks. It was Herkimer the Mad Hermit, but without his shepherd's crook and, instead of shuffling along bent almost double, he was walking erectly but quietly on the balls of his feet. It took the hunter a long moment to realize what else was out of character. Under the hem of the dirty robe the feet striding smartly over the rocks were clad in polished cowboy boots.

He stopped at the top of the rock wall that framed the mesa and brought his hand out of the folds of the gown, holding a most businesslike-looking six-gun. He stood for a full minute, looking down at the shouting pair.

They finally ran out of breath and in the momentary silence he said quietly, "So you finally got back from town, Matt. It's been a long time since you rode in for supplies. We flipped a coin, remember, and I agreed to stay and guard the mine while you made the trip. I did my best, never guessing that the skunk I was guarding it against was you."

They were all gaping up at the weird figure above. The sheriff quietly and very carefully lowered the hammer of his gun and dropped the weapon back into its holster. The skinny man, Matt, obviously the mining engineer who had been the long-missing partner, was the first to recover from shock.

"Herkimer," he bawled. "You dirty crook! You cheat! You sneak thief! Registering a claim on half that mesa top before we ever set out and using a phony name, you scoundrel! I went in good faith to register the mine in both our names, but when I discovered your perfidy, I swore I'd see that you never got a nickel out of that hole in the rock, you skunk."

Herkimer whinnied a high-pitched giggle and squealed, *"Hee-hee!* You'd be the sickest feller on earth if you knew how many 'nickels' I dug outa that hole in the rock before your team of cutthroats moved in. I got more'n enough gold stashed away to keep me on velvet the rest of my life."

"You thief!" the thin man squawled. "Half that gold is mine. I demand my share, including half of what you've already blown."

"You go right ahead and demand it, Matt. But you try grabbin' one ounce and you'll get your arm broke." He whinnied again. "Even if you could find out where it's stashed."

The bounty hunter leaned against the base of the rock spire and chewed his lip in thought. Bits and pieces of the puzzle were coming together but there were still large gaps in the picture. Obviously, the thin man and the sheriff had originally conspired to loot the new mine. But since its ownership was registered in Herkimer's name, they worked out the elaborate ruse of pretending the gold came from a new vein in the Spondulix.

According to the records at the court house, one of the five owners of the Spondulix was a mining engineer by the name of Herbert Rebock, which could very well be an alias of the thin man. How Dan Murthy was pressured into being a party to the scheme was a mystery, but the hunter was positive that the mine superintendent was not a willing participant.

His thoughts were interrupted by the pound of hooves and the rumble of heavy wheels. The freight wagon with its escort of a dozen riders came over a swell of ground and halted abruptly at sight of the group. After an extended conference, one rider detached himself from the group and cautiously approached, his hand on the butt of his holstered gun.

As he drew nearer, the bounty hunter gave a little start of recognition. In the depths of his cash-register mind a bell jangled and a card popped up: *Eddie "Big Butch" Quant—five thousand dollars, dead or alive.*

Down below, the sheriff and the thin man stood frozen in surprise. After a startled moment, Herkimer whirled and scurried out of sight behind one of the rock spires. Only Red Buckley appeared completely at ease. He lifted a hand in greeting.

"Howdy, Butch."

"Hi, Red." The outlaw scowled at the others, then suddenly caught sight of the badge on the sheriff's shirt. He made a grab for his gun, yelling, "A lawman! What the hell is this, a trap?"

"Take it easy, Butch. These are the hombres who set up this whole deal."

Quant glared for a long moment, then slowly let his hand drop from the butt of his gun.

"You better be tellin' the truth, by God, or there are gonna be some corpses strewn around. In case you ain't noticed, you're way outgunned. But anyhow, tin stars always make me nervous. I'd rather do my business with Canuse as usual."

"Butch," Red said by way of explanation, "is one of your best customers."

"Canuse is dead," the sheriff said harshly. "Him and every man of his crew was shot and pitched into the canyon. Herkimer the Hermit stumbled on their bodies at the base of the cliff. He says every last man had a bullet hole square in the middle of his forehead. But that don't mean we're out of business. What have you got, dust or bars?"

Quant scowled at him for the space of several breaths before grunting, "Dust."

"Okay. Have your boys bring it here. Same deal, same payoff."

"Now, hold on a minute," the thin man broke in, his face crimson with anger. "In case you've forgotten, you aren't bossing this deal any longer. *I'm* running it and *I'll* say when we do business and on what terms. You just jump on your little pink pony and flag your butt to hell out of here. And *stay* out."

"Go to hell," the sheriff yelled. "Nobody's runnin' me out or crowdin' me out, you scrawny bag of bluster."

"Shut up, the two of you!" Quant broke in savagely. His gun was in his hand, covering the pair. "If you two want to kill each other it's all right with me, but wait until we're out of here. When partners get into a squabble like this, the scheme is as good as washed, anyhow, whatever you do. So we can find some other way to unload our dust. But before we go, I'm goin' to see just what's at the bottom of the hole with the ladder in it. Canuse wouldn't say, but if it's what I got a hunch it is, me and the boys'll take over."

"I'll tell you what's down there," Red Buckley broke in eagerly.

"Shut up!" the sheriff and the thin man yelled in unison. "You dirty traitor."

"Screw you!" Red yelled back. "I don't owe either one of you one goddam thing. I'll tell you what it is, Butch. It's just only the richest gold mine in the Territory. The vein's so thick and pure you can pick chunks out with a penknife. If you want to take over, me and the boys'll throw in with you. I know every detail of the hot gold operation. I can handle it the same as always for yuh."

"If it's as good as you say, you got a deal, Red."

The bounty hunter nodded grimly to himself. The talk he was hearing cleared up a major part of the Spondulix Mine mystery. With new mines being opened almost weekly, practically every stagecoach and freight wagon carried one or more chests of gold dust or nuggets and the highwaymen were having a field day.

However, the problem of disposing of stolen gold was becoming acute. Most outlaws were too well known to take their plunder to the mint or to a reputable bank. Furthermore, metallurgists and assayers were becoming increasingly efficient in identifying the source of gold by the nature and percentage of various impurities present in the metal, but which vary widely from one mine to another. By shipping stolen gold as the legitimate output of the well-known Spondulix Mine, the operators of the scheme avoided any breath of suspicion while cleaning up a fantastic fortune.

Quant waved his arm in signal and his waiting group instantly surged into motion. As they came closer, the bounty hunter studied a rider in the lead and nodded with satisfaction.

"Cut-Face Cribley," he murmured. "Fifteen hundred."

From somewhere fairly close a gun *blammed*. Cut-Face twisted partway around in the saddle, made a vague, futile grab for the horn, then plunged to the ground to lie unmoving.

The next moment Bloody Hand and his renegade cut-throats came streaming into sight from among the broken rocks that covered the ground to the east. Somehow, probably by theft, the Apaches had procured a motley assortment of horses and ponies to replace those abandoned when they fled from Dollar Sign Canyon. They waved an equally motley assortment of weapons as they charged across the open ground, screeching and howling like fiends from the Pit.

Chapter 18

The shocking appearance of the Apaches brought an abrupt end to the quarreling and feuding. Self-preservation was suddenly the first and only law. Survival would depend upon mutual cooperation in defense.

The sheriff and his slat-thin adversary scrambled up the rock wall shoulder to shoulder, the sheriff yelling, "Everybody take cover among the high rocks."

Red Buckley and his two companions were at their heels. Butch Quant and his men had snatched their rifles from the scabbards and abandoned their horses, to swarm up onto the mesa. The driver of the wagon was tugging at one handle of the gold chest, bawling, "Gimme a hand, you sonsabitches! Gimme a goddam hand!" When no one paid any attention he abandoned the effort, snatched his own rifle from the wagon bed and joined the race to cover.

Dan Murthy, overlooked and weaponless, clambered up the wall and dived behind the nearest sandstone spire. As he ran around the base he came face to face with the bounty hunter. He stared for a startled moment and his jaw dropped.

"You!"

"I got your message," the hunter said. "Finally."

Murthy clutched his arm. "Have you found her?"

"Not yet," the hunter said. "But I've got a pretty good idea where she is."

"If I only had a gun," Murthy moaned. "They took away mine, of course."

"Stay put and I'll get you one. I've got some spares tucked away back here."

By then both men had to shout to be heard above the racketing of guns. The Indians were shooting wildly and, for the most part blindly, the slugs thudding into the soft sandstone or screaming off in ricochets. The embattled

131

whites were firing more cautiously, picking targets and conserving their ammunition. Risking a quick look, the hunter saw several ragged bundles on the ground and riderless horses stampeding.

Ducking back he ran deeper into the mesa, keeping the maze of rock spires between himself and the attacking Apaches. At the camp site Fairfeather was propped on his elbows.

"What the hell's going on?"

"Your friend, Bloody Hand, and his merry companions. He must have somehow gotten wind of rich plunder up here."

Flinging himself prone, he pawed under the overhang and brought out the holstered pistols he had taken from the bodies of Canuse and his crew. With them were three loaded rifles he had taken from their sleeping tunnel. He scrambled up, grabbed out his sheath knife and slashed at the thongs binding the splints to Fairfeather's legs.

"What the hell are you doing, you crazy loony?"

"Here's your gun," the hunter snapped. "Grab yourself a rifle and come on. We need every gun we can get to hold them off."

"You're out of your mind!" Fairfeather howled. "Stinking, babbling crazy! How am I supposed to get there with two broken legs, you idiot—walk on my elbows?"

"Your legs are no more broken than mine. They were badly bruised and twisted but I couldn't feel any broken bones. I only said that to keep you from trying to collect your own bounty. I had more important things to do than go around with my chin over my shoulder, watching for a backshooter." He draped the gun-belts over his shoulder and dropped one of the rifles beside the stunned Fairfeather. "Come on. Get up and stamp around. Your legs will be all right, once you get the circulation started again. Or should I go out and politely ask Bloody Hand to hold off his attack until you feel up to joining us?"

Fairfeather cursed him wildly. He pushed himself to a sitting position and cautiously moved first one leg and then the other.

"That's more like it," the hunter said. "Now rear up and try putting one foot in front of the other. With luck you may make it before Bloody Hand gets a chance to tie each foot to a different horse and drive the horses in opposite directions."

He turned and ran back toward the sound of battle. Murthy was crouching, peering around the edge of the rock. He sprang up, his eyes wide, to snatch the gun-belt and rifle the hunter held out.

"Now," he said, buckling on the belt, "I can begin to feel like a man again. Luckily, I'm a left-hander so I'll stick to the left side of the rock."

"I'm going upstairs," the hunter said. "All this racket and ruckus down here makes my ears ring."

Murthy paused in the act of bringing the rifle to his shoulder.

"If you should come out of this and I don't, promise me you'll try to find her."

"I'll do my best," the hunter said. "Your wife?"

"My daughter. Her mother died when she was born. At first they'd bring me a piece of her clothing every little while, to prove they had her and then to remind me of what would happen to her if I didn't keep their secret and do what I was told. Then they suddenly stopped doing that for some reason and acted terribly upset about something. I don't know what was wrong, but it's got me worried sick."

"I think I know the reason and it isn't what you imagine. But we'd better pitch in and get this war won if you ever expect to find her."

A man ran around behind an adjoining rock spire, using its bulk as a shield while he reloaded his pistol. It took the hunter a long moment to recognize the figure as Herkimer.

He had discarded the dirty white robe along with his stoop and stood vigorously erect in a suit of finely tailored broadcloth, with a watch chain of gold nuggets looped across the flowered vest. Only the unkempt tangle of white hair and whiskers remained to link the natty H. K. Highcomer to the bent and shuffling recluse of Dollar Sign Canyon.

Herkimer was so completely absorbed in the excitement of the struggle that the brief glance he threw toward the hunter and Dan Murthy held no sign of recognition. He finished reloading, snapped the cylinder of the gun back into the frame and darted out of sight around the rock.

For his cover, the hunter had deliberately selected one of the shorter truncated spires of sandstone with a flat top and a broken, sloping side that made for easier climbing. It took him no more than a few minutes to clamber to the top. He bellied across to the front edge and cautiously peered over.

It was obvious at first glance that while Bloody Hand's reputation for savagery was probably well deserved, he would earn few accolades as a military technician. Apparently his strategy was to whip up his followers to a blind frenzy and charge straight in, trusting to their ferocious appearance and savage yells to unnerve their victims. In this case, the tactic proved to be a monumental misjudgment. A score or more of dead or badly wounded Apaches and a number of horses were scattered over the open ground below the mesa's rock wall, testimony to the deadly accurate fire of the defenders.

The Indians were grouped just out of gun range, being harangued by a stocky horseman whom the bounty hunter felt certain was Bloody Hand himself. He was apparently working them up to another suicidal charge. The sound of his shouting came faintly to the hunter's ears.

From his elevated perch he could look down at perhaps half the defenders. The sheriff and his cadaverous erstwhile enemy shared an adjoining rock. The sheriff was using Fairfeather's fancy rifle with the telescope sight and had apparently given the hunter's Winchester to the thin man. Just beyond, Red Buckley and his two companions shared a rock adjoining one that sheltered Butch Quant and one of his men. For the moment, there was no firing. The only sound was the clack and clatter of hurried checking and reloading.

A sudden wild screeching and howling erupted. The Apaches were coming in in another stubborn suicidal charge. Down below somewhere a single rifle shot blasted.

The sheriff's voice bawled, "Hold your fire, you goddam idiot! Hold your fire until they're so close you can't miss. When we run out of ammunition, there ain't goin' to be time to send somebody to town for a new supply."

A second shot sounded, this one from behind the line of defenders. The hunter squirmed around far enough to see Fairfeather standing between raised up rock spires, swaying a bit but holding his rifle ready for another shot. The body of an Apache, almost naked and weirdly painted, sprawled on the rocky ground a few yards away.

"What happened?" the hunter called.

"He was ready to plug the man down below you there

in the back when I blew him out from under his topknot. If it had been *your* back you can be damn sure I wouldn't have interfered."

"That's what I like," the hunter said. "A man who minds his own business and lets others mind theirs."

A ragged volley of gunfire whirled his attention to the front. The charging Indians were close enough to open fire with a ragtag assortment of weapons, ranging from bows and arrows to ancient flintlock muskets to a few modern rifles. The defenders were opening a return fire with murderous effect.

The bounty hunter fired twice and had the satisfaction of seeing two fiercely painted figures topple from their horses. He jacked another shell into the breech, then held his fire, staring narrow-eyed at the attackers. It seemed to him that the number of charging Apaches had dwindled sharply—much more, in fact, than could be accounted for by their mounting casualties. He searched the line in vain for a sight of the red turban that identified Bloody Hand.

The charging line was swiftly disintegrating, the surviving Apaches whirling their mounts and racing back out of range of the deadly return fire. The bounty hunter suddenly flung himself around and scrambled to the rear edge of his crow's nest perch. He caught a glimpse of savagely painted figures flitting from cover to cover, back beyond the point where the dead Apache lay sprawled. Apparently, Bloody Hand was not quite such an inept tactician after all. He fired and one of the shadowy phantoms fell and lay still.

From below, the voice of the sheriff bawled, "Hold fire, dammit to hell! Can't you see their charge is broken?"

"That charge was a feint," the hunter shouted back. "Guard your backs. Bloody Hand and his main force are coming at you from behind on foot."

Butch Quant burst into sight, his rifle at the ready. His big head swiveled from side to side.

"Where are they? Show me the bastards! I'll teach 'em not to try to steal Butch Quant's gold dust, damn 'em!" His voice climbed to a bellow. "Where are you, Bloody Hand, you big fake? You been claimin' you're the most feared outlaw in the Territory. Come out and prove it, man-to-man, if you ain't the coward I know you for."

A savagely painted figure in a red turban stepped from behind one of the rock spires with his rifle to his shoulder.

He fired once. Butch Quant uttered what sounded like a high-pitched giggle, spun around on his toes like an elephant practicing ballet and slammed to the ground.

The bounty hunter's rifle blasted, the sound of the shot merging with that of another shot from directly below. Bloody Hand was flung backward against the rock by the impact of two high-powered slugs. He rebounded, teetered for a moment, dropped his rifle and fell on it.

The bounty hunter was already scrambling recklessly down the slope of the rock spire. At the bottom he almost collided with Fairfeather, who squawled, "No, you don't! He's all mine! I shot him and I claim the bounty. My shot was a second ahead of yours, damn you!"

"The hell it was," the hunter snapped. "You wouldn't have had a rifle, or even been here, if it wasn't for me. He's my kill and I'm cashing him in."

Fairfeather's eyes narrowed. His rifle, tight against his hip, swung until its muzzle was centered on the hunter's chest.

"Come to think of it," the fake reverend said through his clenched teeth, "I'm cashing in *two* bounties—three, including Butch Quant. Now that I know I'm not a helpless cripple, depending on you for survival, there's not a reason in the world why I don't kill you right now for that fifty thousand."

The bounty hunter burst into a roar of unfeigned laughter.

Chapter 19

Fairfeather stared at the hunter, his jaw slack. "If dying is so almighty funny, I should have amused you a long time ago."

Still choked with laughter, the hunter said. "It isn't the dying that's so funny. It's you figuring on a reward you'll never collect. You remember that small-time character you cashed in a while back—Bad-Luck Beals? Now that he's dead, you could take over his nickname. It'd fit you like a glove." He strangled on another paroxysm of laughter. "Bad-Luck Fairfeather. Or, better yet because it sounds better, Foul-Luck Fairfeather."

"If you've got some big news to spill, spit it out, because your time is getting damn short."

"In some ways, friend, you're sorrier than a skunk with an empty sack when the hound dogs have been let loose. You dream up this wild scheme of a huge bounty on me. But when you set out to get cash backing, you wind up hung on a cactus. You get out of that situation, take a shot at me and grab yourself a butt full of rocks. Once you've finally got me cold and dead, who's going to pay that rich bounty?"

"The Organized Outlaws Association, damn you."

"Hooray," the hunter said. "And let's see if I remember the big contributing members of the Organized Outlaws. There was the McKean Brothers, shot to death ten days ago in a sheriff's ambush outside Nogales, in case you hadn't heard the news. Then there was Mitch Magruder and Skull Scarson, both of whom I cashed in two-three weeks back. Bart Sigmund, shot to death holding up a Wells Fargo stagecoach. Wall-Eye Willis, who forgot to duck when a deputy's bullet with his name on it came whistling by. It appears, my friend, that your top backers have very short life-spans. Now your remaining major backers have conveniently come to you—Bloody Hand

137

right over there and Butch Quant over here. So go ahead and kill me and see who is left to pay you even the cost of the bullet it took."

Fairfeather cursed wildly and yelled, "Then I'll do it for my own satisfaction, you stinking louse. After what you did to me, I . . ."

A painted figure burst from behind a rock and leaped at him, swinging a hand axe and waving a thick-bladed scalping knife. Fairfeather swung the rifle up horizontally in both hands and caught both weapons against the barrel. Before the Indian could recover, the hunter fired from the hip, the slug smashing into the painted back between the shoulder blades.

Fairfeather yelled, "What the hell are you trying to do, buy your life by nursemaiding mine? I can take care of myself."

"You damn well better," the hunter yelped as a dozen or more of the painted savages burst from behind the rocks to leap on them.

He got off two shots that blasted two of the attackers before they swarmed over him, struggling to wrest the rifle from his hands. Fairfeather was on his knees, struggling to cling to his weapon and use it to ward off a swinging axe. All up and down the line he glimpsed hand-to-hand struggles with the Apache attackers.

An Indian had both hands on the muzzle of his rifle and was jerking and twisting it furiously in an effort to wrest it loose. The hunter was attempting to use his greater strength to bring the muzzle into line with the Apache's belly, but each time he moved the rifle, the Indian moved with it, keeping just out of line. Grunting, tugging, panting, they circled like dancers in a slow-motion minuet.

A shot rang out. The Apache let go of the rifle barrel and tumbled backward, the whole top of his shaven skull a gory welter. Fairfeather, on his feet and momentarily free of attackers, held his rifle in his left hand and used his right to tuck the long-barreled pistol back into his waistband.

"That makes us even on that score," he growled. "Now I don't owe you any favors, so don't expect any."

The clear space between the rocks was suddenly swarming with new attackers, howling like wolves. Conserving his dwindling ammunition supply, the bounty hunter reversed his rifle and swung it as a club. From the corner of his eye he glimpsed Fairfeather employing the same tactic.

Above the savage screeching he heard the ripe-melon sound of a splitting skull. A powerfully built Apache rushed at him with a scalping knife poised high. The hunter drove the butt of his rifle into the Indian's belly, then smashed it full into the painted face, feeling teeth and jawbone give way. He realized suddenly that he and Fairfeather were fighting almost back-to-back.

Flailing the rifle as a club, he drove through the swarm of attackers to where the body of Bloody Hand lay almost hidden in the deep shadow of a rock. Dropping the rifle he caught the dead chief by his rawhide string belt and throat and swung it high above his head.

"Look!" he roared in a stentorian voice that boomed its echoes off the rocks. "Look at your great leader now. You have followed him for a long time. You know where he has gone now. Are you eager to follow him to that place, too?"

With a mighty heave he sent the corpse flying out into the center of the clear space for all the attackers to see. There was a startled silence, then the savage howling gave way to a chorus of wails. Clearly, most of the Apaches had been unaware of their leader's death.

Two Indians ran out, caught up the corpse of Bloody Hand between them and raced out of sight among the rocks. Suddenly other Indians were melting away until, with startling abruptness, there was not an Apache in sight.

"By God," Fairfeather panted, leaning on his rifle for support, "you pulled it off. I never thought it would work, but it did."

The hunter looked around and sucked in a sharp breath.

"That isn't all that's been pulled off here. In case you hadn't noticed, we seem to have this mesa all to ourselves—unless the others were all killed, which is highly unlikely."

A hasty search of the rocks turned up two bodies—one of Quant's men and one of Red Buckley's two hardcase companions. Even Herkimer had disappeared. Neither of the two dead men had merited a bounty so they were left where they fell to enrich the lives of the vultures.

The hunter scrambled back up to the flat top of the truncated spire. There was no one in sight but northward a cloud of dust was moving up the trail to the Spondulix Mine. The hunter snatched his spy glass from its clip inside his poncho, snapped it open and focussed on the base of the dust cloud. He swore softly but fervently under his breath.

Racing up the trail was the wagon carrying Butch Quant's stolen gold dust, the team lashed to a dead run. The surviving members of Quant's band surrounded the wagon. Riding ahead were the sheriff and the thin man with Dan Murthy between them. Apparently the two rivals had patched up some kind of truce between them rather than let their fantastically profitable scheme collapse.

The bounty hunter scrambled back down. "We've really been played for suckers. While we were fighting off the Apaches . . ."

He stopped short, staring around the empty mesa. Fairfeather was nowhere to be seen. He had vanished into thin air, and with him had vanished the five-thousand-dollar corpse of Big Butch Quant. The twenty-thousand-dollar body of Bloody Hand had already been relinquished as a sacrifice to end the Apache attack. That left the bounty hunter only one avenue of profit for a long, arduous and dangerous undertaking.

After showing Fairfeather the two pokes of raw gold, he had waited until the injured man dozed off, then had prudently moved the entire store of pokes to a new hiding place some distance away. The sheriff had mentioned the vicinity of seventy thousand dollars, which was not at all a bad vicinity in which to be caught.

He ran among the spires, guiding himself along a twisting path by the weird rock formations. He arrived presently at a spire with a narrow crevasse at the base. Flinging himself down he shoved his hand into the crevasse. For a long moment he was utterly motionless. Then he began to scrabble wildly into the space, shoving his arm in to the shoulder.

"You lookin' for something, son?" Herkimer asked.

He was leaning against the rock, looking mildly interested and faintly amused. The hunter snatched his arm out and glared up at the incongruous figure.

"So you've had your fun. So where the hell are they?"

"*They?*" Herkimer said. "Oh—oh, you mean the pokes full of raw gold. Why didn't you say so? You young fellers think so fast your heads zip-zip from here to there and damn if an old coot like me can keep up with it. Why, son, I watched you drag 'em out of that other place and tote 'em over here. Worked like a dog you did, grunting and sweating. Felt right sorry for you, I did. But after you'd went I got to thinkin' this ain't the safest hidin' place. So I lugged 'em all to a better place where no thief could ever find 'em."

"Now that," the hunter said through his teeth, "is just about the kindest, nicest thing anybody ever did for me and you have no idea how much I appreciate it. I know the responsibility must be a heavy load to bear, so if you'll tell me where that safer place is, or lead me to it, I'll be glad to take the load off your back."

"Dawggone," Herkimer said, rasping his fingernails through the tangle of whiskers. "Dawggone, boy, but I wish you hadn't said that. You just reminded me that no matter how young I feel, I must be gettin' old because my memory's fadin'. Do you know, I've tried and tried and tried to remember where I put them gold pokes and I'm everlastin'ly blessed if I can. It's gone clean out of my mind, seems like."

"I had a feeling you might suffer a loss of memory, but I've got just the thing to cure it," the hunter said grimly.

His hand darted under the poncho to the butt of his gun and froze there. Herkimer's hand seemed barely to move, but suddenly the swivel holster was tilted up, the muzzle of the pistol peeping through its open bottom pointing straight at the hunter's middle.

"Uh-uh-uh!" Herkimer said sadly. "That's the hull trouble with you youngsters today. Too goldang impetuous. Can't never seem to wait for dee-velopments to dee-velop natural. Got to push, push, push all the time. You know, I got me a feelin' you're just itchin' to ride into town or up to the Spondulix and start smashin' things up, just for the hell of it. Yuh know how I can tell, son? Because I got me the same goldern urge. Now, if you was to let me lope along with you and get me a piece o' the fun, too, it's just possible the smell of gunpowder smoke might stir up that goldang lazy memory of mine into rememberin' where them pokes o' gold is hid."

"You ring-tailed faker! All right. You can ride along on one condition—that you drop that phony accent and talk straight."

Herkimer heaved a deep sigh. "You drive a mighty hard bargain, son, but what can a poor, helpless old man do but accept your terms?"

In its heyday, the office of the Spondulix resembled an elegant gentlemen's club, as befitted the richest mine in the Territory. Visitors waded ankle deep across an imported rug to reach an enormous mahogany flat-topped desk, or sank into luxurious overstuffed chairs to await a summons to Dan Murthy's inner sanctum.

Since the vein petered out and the mine closed, however, the lounge had fallen on evil days. The rug was matted now with dried manure, caked mud and rock dust. Vandals had broken half the windows, slashed the overstuffed chairs and carved obscene graffiti on the mahogany desk top. Spiders, lizards and pack rats had taken up residence.

Nevertheless, at the moment, it held a faint counterpart of the great executive councils it had housed in a grander past. The thin man sat hunched over the mahogany desk, filling in the spaces on a printed form, using a dog-eared paper as a guide. He was using a goose quill pen and pausing every few strokes to sharpen it delicately with a gold-cased penknife.

"Those new steel pens," he muttered under his breath, "are an abomination. Progress—*gahhh!*"

The sheriff was on his feet, leaning on the desk and bending far over to peer at what the thin man was writing. Murthy sat in a corner, his complexion the color of wet ashes, clenched fists resting on his knees, the knuckles stark white. Across the room Red Buckley sat bolt upright in a broken chair, his face nearly as ashen as that of the mine superintendent.

The thin man finished, laid down the quill pen and waved the paper in the air to dry the ink. The sheriff snatched it out of his hands. He studied it through narrowed eyes, shaking his head.

"My God, what a job. I have to give you credit, Ash, or whatever you call yourself now. Any circuit judge in the Territory would record this without question as a genuine bill of sale, signed by H. K. Highcomer, transferring full and inclusive ownership of the Dollar Sign gold mine to the D & K Syndicate, with you and me as full and equal owners. And it better, by God, stay that way, you crooked bastard."

"Now, now, Ben, I thought we'd agreed to bury the hatchet and start over."

"That we did," the sheriff said grimly, "but don't let me catch you makin' out one of these phony bills of sale for *my* interest to you or I'll bury the hatchet right in your doublecrossing skull, you bastard. But just the same, you did one helluva job on this. It's a perfect copy of the old galoot's signature and handwriting."

"If I do say so myself," the thin man said modestly, "forgery is one of my finest natural talents." He chuckled. "How else do you think I acquired my certificate as a duly licensed mining engineer, approved by the U. S. Bureau of Mines, without ever completing the sixth grade?"

"Oh, you're a real genius," the sheriff said sourly. "So what happens now? You got a bill of sale, transferring the mine to us, but we've still got that damn old coot running around, ready to deny his signature."

The thin man waved airily. "Absolutely no sweat, partner. Red Buckley, here, is going to see to it that Herkimer suddenly stops running around and becomes very, very dead. That's part of the price he's agreed to pay for our overlooking his turning snake-in-the-grass down there on the mesa this morning. Isn't that the size of it, Red?"

"Yes," Red said hoarsely, then changed his reply hastily to, "Yes, *sir.*"

"You see, Ben," the thin man said suavely, "I didn't actually agree to forgive or forget his dirty sellout, but I agreed to overlook it as long as he did his job and remained at least openly faithful."

"Oh, I can understand that, *partner.* I feel the same way about you."

"Oh, cut it out," Red Buckley growled sullenly. "Goddammit, where would any of us be if we stuck with the losers? And you sure looked like prime losers down there on the mesa when Big Butch laid it down. If the Apaches hadn't busted in right then, you would be, too, so don't get so goddam high and mighty with me. You're each bustin' your empty balls to doublecross the other, first chance you get."

"That's the exciting thing about these deals," the thin man said. "You're kept on your toes every moment, knowing you could be dead the moment you relax your vigilance. Which, by the way, Ben, I never do."

The door crashed open and the surviving companion of

Red Buckley burst in, wild-eyed, clutching a collapsible telescope.

"They're comin'," he panted. "No more'n a mile down the trail. That bounty killer in the Mex night shirt and that old coot with the white hair and whiskers. They're joggin' down the trail, lookin' as sweet as this morning's cream, headin' right straight for here."

"That puts you in business, Red," the thin man said. "Go kill them both, but make sure you kill Herkimer first. He's the one we can't afford to leave alive if we're to take over the richest mine in the Territory."

"Leave me out of it," the sheriff yelled. "I'm duckin' outa here the back way. I can't do anybody any good if I'm to get tied into a swindle deal. I got to stay with my skirts as clean as can be to bail you out if it gets rough."

"Skirts," the thin man said sarcastically, "on you they would look just perfect—especially if they had a yellow belly-band."

"Keep asking for it," the sheriff panted furiously, "and I'll get back to give it to you."

He slammed out the back door of the mine office, untied his horse, leaped into the saddle and spurred off in the direction of San Quenada.

Down the trail the hunter said, "Judging by that dust cloud, we spooked one of 'em real good and, for my money, it's got to be that cute sheriff, Ben Dobrin. So be it."

Chapter 20

"You watch me, Mace," Red Buckley told his companion. "You watch real good and you'll learn things. They don't call me Bang-Bang Buckley for nothin'. When you want to get rid of somebody quick and permanent, there's nothin' beats dynamite. You shoot a man and less'n you hit him dead center, he can still draw and blow your head off. But you give him the big bang and you don't even have to hit him to scatter him from hell to breakfast and halfways back."

"I'm watchin', Red," Mace said nervously, "but I couldn't never be as smart as you. Besides, that stuff scares the pants off me, just bein' around it."

"Once you learn how to handle it proper," Red said smugly, "it's as safe as a baby's rattle. You watch how I do it."

He got a stick of dynamite out of a wooden box that was nearly full, a copper fulminate cap from a smaller box and cut a short length of fuse from a coil. The man called Mace was pushed as far back as their tight pocket in the rocks permitted and his forehead glistened with liquid fright.

Red threaded the length of fuse, fitted the blasting cap over the end of the dynamite stick and crimped it tight with his teeth. He set the prepared stick on the rock rim, fished out a stump of partly-smoked cigar and dragged a kitchen match to light across the rock. Mace squawked and crowded back even further, his eyes wild.

"Watch it, Red! For God's sake, watch it with that match. You wanna blow us both to kingdom come?"

Red finished lighting the cigar stump and gusted out a smoke-laden laugh. He blew out the match and tossed it away.

"You *are* the Nervous Nelly, ain't you?" He got out his knife, hacked off a six-inch length from the coil of fuse and lit it from the cigar stub. He held it, sputtering and throwing sparks, until it had burned almost to his finger-tips, then he tossed it over the rock rim and down into the trail to the Spondulix. "You see, kid, the stuff's as safe as candy to handle when you know what you're doin'."

"And I know somethin' even safer," Mace said sourly. *"Not* handlin' it."

Red chuckled. He leaned out over the rock rim, peering southward, then ducked back.

"Quiet, Mac. They're almost in throwin' range right now."

The hunter finished lighting one of his short *cigarros,* blew out the match and tossed it aside. Herkimer was deep in a longwinded recital of adventures and misadven-tures.

The bounty hunter sniffed and suddenly barked, "Pipe down and keep your eyes open. I get a strong odor of fresh burned powder, and it smells to me more like blasting powder than gunpowder."

They both saw it and yelled at the same time as a brownish-gray cylinder wrapped in greased paper came arching out from among the rocks, spitting sparks and trailing a plume of smoke. The horses shied as the object landed in the middle of the trail almost under their hooves.

Herkimer yelled and yanked at the reins, trying to swing his mount back and away from the deadly menace. The hunter's hand flashed under the poncho and out again, holding his gun. The gun blasted and a half-inch of sputtering fuse whipped away from the dynamite stick, leaving another half-inch still unburned.

The hunter flung himself out of the saddle, snatched up the stick and lit the remaining stub of fuse from his *cigarro.* As it sputtered to life he hurled it with deadly accuracy into the pocket of rocks from whence it had come.

A wild yell of pure terror rose and was lost in the crash of the dynamite blast. This, in turn, was engulfed in an earth-shaking thunder as the boxes of dynamite and blast-ing caps blew up.

In the Spondulix office, the thin man shook his head admiringly and murmured, "That Buckley. He's a rat, but when he sets out to blow somebody up, he never uses half measures."

San Quenada boasted the largest jail in the Territory. As usual, it was jammed with horsethieves, cattle rustlers, highwaymen, killers and assorted malefactors. The sheriff was always assiduous in jailing the smaller offenders and those who stubbornly remained uncooperative. Now, with the fall elections coming up, he was even more diligent than usual.

He flung himself out of the saddle, ran into his office and snatched a heavy ring of keys from a nail. He burst into the jail annex in the rear and ran along the corridor, unlocking the cell doors.

"I've got a job for you fellers," he shouted above the tumult of questions. "A full pardon and a cash bonus to boot. I'm deputizing you all. Raise your right hands and say, 'I swear.' "

A short, fat, swarthy man said anxiously, "Swear *what*, sheriff?"

"What the hell difference does it make? Just swear!"

"Okay," the fat man said amiably. "Goddam to bitchin' hell."

"That'll do," the sheriff yelled. "In here to get your badges and guns."

He got out a box of deputy badges and threw it on the desk, then got a key to unlock the gun cabinet. He brought out rifles and pistol belts and piled them on the desk.

"Hey, sheriff," the fat man said anxiously, "who we got a fight with anyhow? The U. S. Army?"

"Two men, Arnie," the sheriff said. "And one of 'em's an old, white-haired codger who won't give you any trouble. He's just an old nuisance to be got rid of. The other one's younger and tougher, but he's still only one man against ..." he paused, wagging a stubby finger as he counted heads, "ten-eleven. One man against eleven and what better odds could anybody ask? Besides, you got a whole empty town to ambush him in."

"How we know this one, eh?" the fat man demanded. "Maybe we make mistake, kill the wrong man."

"You'll know this one. He wears a Mex poncho that hangs down to his heels ..."

The fat man threw badge and gun back on the desk.

"*Oh,* no! Maybe, like they say, next week I hang for horsethief but I rather take chance on gallows than against *him.*"

He marched back to the jail wing, went into his cell and firmly slammed the barred door behind him.

There was a scrabbling at the door of the mine office and the thin man yelled, "Come on it! Come in, Red, and let's hear the details."

The door flew open and Herkimer said, "Doesn't it beat hell how you simply can't hang onto help these days? Now, you take Red and his pal, whatever his name is—*was*—for example. All of a sudden the pair of them take off, like they're flying to the moon. Not even a word of goodbye. Just fly all to pieces and away they go. They're just too dang temperamental, I'd guess."

The thin man put unsteady hands on the desk top.

"H-Hello, Herk, old fella. It's kind of like old times, you and me together. It's just too bad Petey can't be with us. He was a real card, that old desert rat."

"He sure was," Herkimer said. "I keep seein' him there on the floor of that cave with his head twisted clean around and under him. It makes me laugh and laugh, fit to be tied. In a way Petey was a lot like me. We both missed out on a goldang fortune, one way or another."

"Oh, but you didn't miss out, Herk. That's the big surprise I tucked away for you, fella. Half of every nickel I got out of that mine, I put away for you, old boy. Now you've got that hand hanging over your gun like a real slinger and you know damn well you never could find your gun in a big hurry, even if all the candles were lit in the house. So be smart and don't crowd me into doing something I'll be sorry for for the rest of my life."

"That," Herkimer said, "is going to be one of the shortest sorry periods they ever recorded. You want to take it like that, settin' down, or do you want to stand up first and make like you got a grabbin' chance?" He snickered in the voice of the mad hermit of Dollar Sign Canyon. "All them weeks and months and years I waited for you to come back, you guess what I did to pass away the time. I *practiced*, old partner. I done that draw-and-fire business until I could spit tobaccky and blow it to blazes before it hit the ground. Then I figgered out a way to get even faster. You want to see how it's done? Just grab for your iron and I'll show you."

Sweat glistened on the thin man's forehead. "Now wait,

Herk. Just take it easy. This is something we can talk over like reasonable men ..."

He was no slouch of a gunman. He had his revolver half cleared when Herkimer tipped the swivel holster up and shot him through the heart. The thin man fell across the desk. Herkimer snatched the forged bill of sale from under the body before the blood could soak it. He studied the paper, shaking his head and making small clucking noises.

"I'll be goldanged. According to this here, I went and sold him my gold mine, but I sure don't remember it. If I did I musta been drunk as a skunk at the time."

The bounty hunter leaned in the door.

"Killing one rat doesn't wipe out the breed. Are you going to spend the night here admiring your handiwork, or are you coming with me to stir up some more trouble?"

As Herkimer started for the door, Dan Murthy jumped to his feet.

"Wait! They took away those guns you gave me this morning, but if I can find another I'd like to go with you."

The hunter dipped a hand under the poncho and brought out an extra pistol.

"Here. Catch and join the party." He tossed the gun to the superintendent, who caught it deftly and gratefully. "You'll have to dig up your own spare bullets, though. I'm just about cleaned out."

"*One* bullet is all I'll need," Murthy said through his teeth.

Outside, the hunter asked, "Any idea where we might find you a horse?"

"Mine should be with the others, picketed in a glade behind the stamp mill. Give me two minutes to saddle up."

The hunter studied Herkimer through narrowed eyes.

"Are you sure you don't want to change your story about the girl, or add anything to it?"

Murthy whirled and grabbed Herkimer's arm.

"Does he mean my daughter? Where is she? Is she all right?"

"I don't know and that's the straight truth. I only know I was spying on 'em one day when that crooked sheriff and his redheaded gunhand went into one of those empty shanties in Spondulix and came out carrying what looked like part of a woman's dress. After they left I peeked in and there was a pile of woman's clothes on the floor. I swiped every bit, figuring whatever their game was, having it come up missing would give them conniption fits."

"It nearly drove them out of their minds," Murthy said. "And me, too, worrying about what might have happened to her."

"Maybe your worries are almost over. What could be a more logical place to hold her prisoner than in one of those ghost town shanties? Herkimer's finding her clothing there makes me sure of it."

"Herkimer?" Murthy said, frowning. "Isn't that the same name as the one they call the Mad Hermit?"

"Same name," Herkimer said, chuckling, "same fella." He described his ruse to survive among the savage Apaches. "I found me a neat hideaway above the canyon where I kept my horse and money and city clothes. When I wanted to get away, all I had to do was change, comb out my hair and whiskers and I was the rich H. K. Highcomer."

Chapter 21

In the shadowy interior of the Spondulix Livery Stable, Sheriff Ben Dobrin gave his ragtag "posse" a last-minute briefing. They were a fierce-looking crew, every man wearing a six-gun and carrying a rifle. In addition, several had added Bowie knives to their arsenals.

"Of course," the sheriff was saying, "they might not show up at all. That bang we heard on the way out could have been Red Buckley blowing 'em both to hell, but we can't take chances. The one with no name's had the devil's luck in dodging death traps. If they *are* alive and head for San Quenada, there's no reason they wouldn't take the regular road right down the main street, here. You fellows hole up in those empty shanties that front on the street and keep out of sight until they come abreast, then blow 'em out of their saddles. I want both of 'em dead—stone, cold *dead!*"

"Where'll you be, sheriff?" an eagle-beaked man demanded.

"Right up front here with the doors ajar so I can take a hand if you boys run into any trouble. Now pick your places and stay out of sight."

When they had gone, he eased the stable's wide front doors a couple of inches ajar and settled down on an upturned wooden bucket with his eye to the slit and his rifle across his lap. He almost hoped the pair had escaped any other traps so that he could have the satisfaction of seeing both of them blasted to shreds by the concentrated fire of ten rifles—eleven, counting his own.

At the edge of town the bounty hunter reined in and sat staring along the silent street through narrowed eyes. His two companions had also pulled up and were staring from the hunter to the rows of shanties and back, frowning.

"Well, what are we waiting for?" Herkimer demanded

151

impatiently. "Being a ghost town, are you expecting maybe to see a ghost?"

"Maybe," the hunter said shortly without moving on. "Tell me, wasn't it around noon today that we got some gusty wind?"

"We sure did," Herkimer said. "It blowed like all hell for maybe twenty-thirty minutes, then dropped to a whisper like it does so often at this time of year. Why?"

"I'm wondering how those livery stable doors could stay ajar instead of being blown wide open and half off their hinges by a gusty west wind. I'm also kind of curious about why three shacks on the right side of the street have their shutters open wide, while most of the others are shut tight."

"By damn," Herkimer said. "You don't miss a trick, do yuh, son? I've heard of an eagle eye, but you'd drive an eagle crazy."

"You know this place," the hunter said to Murthy. "Do these shanties have back doors?"

"Sure. How else would people get to their johnnies in time if they had a real rush call? Why? You got an idea?"

"Not too good a one, but it'll have to do."

He sketched his idea briefly. The others nodded and swung off their horses. Leaving them ground-haltered at the end of the street, they drew and cocked their guns and tramped down the rear of the shanties to the three with the open shutters.

Behind the stable doors the sheriff pounded a clenched fist against his thigh and muttered, "Damn you, damn you, oh, damn you, you lucky bastard! There's no doubt at all but what you've got the devil himself as your guardian angel."

Each of the trio was poised behind one of the back doors with one foot lifted. At a signal from the bounty hunter each launched a mighty kick. As the three doors crashed open, each man dived in, bent low and gun blazing. There was a sporadic rattle of return fire but the ex-prisoners were too unnerved by the unexpected assault to aim.

Across the street the sheriff was on his feet, swearing helplessly. He heard the deafening burst of gunfire, followed by an ominous silence. Whirling, he burst out the rear door of the stable and ran as if his life depended upon

In the first of the three shanties the hunter hurdled a pile of bodies and reached the open front window in time to see the sheriff vanish into a tumbledown cottage at the very edge of town. He scrambled out the window as Herkimer and Murthy hurdled the low sills of the other shanty windows to join him.

"Come on," he barked. "The sheriff just dived into that house over there. I'll bet dollars to doughnuts it's where your daughter is being held, but don't rush in or you might set off a panic reaction that would bring her harm."

They trotted toward the cottage, the hunter and Herkimer reloading as they ran. Murthy, afire with impatience, was far ahead and increasing his lead. He stopped short when the voice of the sheriff hailed him from an open window.

"That's far enough, Dan. Hold it right there. I've got a gun to her head and if you come any closer or try any tricks, I'll pull the trigger. The same goes for your friends."

"Patty," the superintendent cried hoarsely. "Can you hear me? Are you all right?"

"Yes, daddy," a girl's voice replied, "but he isn't bluffing. He does have a gun against my head and I'm s-sure he'd do what he says."

Murthy turned a haggard face to his companions.

"What can I do now?"

"Try to bargain with him," the hunter said softly. "Find out what he wants."

"I heard that," the sheriff shouted. "You're a smart man, Nameless. I want out of here without interference and a twenty-four-hour head start. If there aren't any tricks, I'll leave your daughter close to a telegraph office so she can get in touch with you. That ought to be fair enough. What I need now is time."

A new voice from inside said coldly, "Your time just ran out, sheriff . . . or, I should say, *ex*-sheriff."

There were two shots in swift succession, followed by a thud that jarred the cottage. The front door opened and Leemon Fairfeather, still holding the long-barreled pistol, stepped to the threshold.

"It's all over. He's dead and your daughter's safe."

A squealing girl of perhaps seventeen or eighteen rushed past him and threw herself into her father's arms, sobbing with hysterical relief. She was swathed from head to toe in a scabrous blanket.

Fairfeather finished reloading his gun and strolled out, grinning. He tucked the elongated weapon into his waistband over the left hip, positioned for a lightning-swift cross-belly draw.

"What the hell are you doing here?" the hunter growled. "I thought you did a run-out with the body of Butch Quant."

"Oh, I'll cash him in, never you fear," Fairfeather said airily. "Sorry to rob you of that profit but that's the way it comes out sometimes."

"That's quite all right," the hunter said. "It just intrigues me, how many times one supposedly-smart man can foul himself up, totally and completely. Let's see—you cooked up that real cute super-bounty on me and then helped kill off the backers who would pay it. Wasn't that silly? Then you took a shot at me and had the vibrations knock half the cliff down on you. Now you've loused it up again. You're a born loser, pal."

"What the hell do you mean, I've loused it up again?"

"Why," the hunter said equably, "you've got the corpus of good old Butch Quant. But who pays the bounty? Why, the gallant sheriff of San Quenada County, who just happens to be lying dead in there. By whose quick-trigger hand, do you reckon? So now you'll have to wait for a by-election to select the new sheriff, which will take considerable time and by then Butch is going to get god-awful ripe—unless you can find a cooperative ice house."

"So how goddam smart are *you,* wise guy?" Fairfeather yelled. "I at least got me a corpse to collect on. What the hell have *you* got to show for the time you wasted? I figured out all the angles, same as you did, and I realized you weren't being just a Good Samaritan. You were out to cash in, but I just outsmarted you. I added up all the things you let slip here and there, and it led me straight to the Spondulix Mine and then here. So I get here just in time to save Murthy's daughter. And don't think he won't show his appreciation."

Still holding his daughter in his arms, Murthy swung around.

"You're absolutely right, my friend. I only regret that I was financially wiped out when the Spondulix failed and closed. Otherwise, I'd show my appreciation in a far more practical way. But I assure you, sir, my undying gratitude will go with you, even to the ends of the earth."

The hunter seized Murthy's hand and pumped it warmly. "You have no idea how deeply my friend appreciates that. He is simply too choked up with emotion at the moment to speak."

A few yards away Herkimer was doubled over, apparently in the throes of a spasm of some kind. Fairfeather, his face beet-red in color, glared fiercely at the hunter.

"Don't look so goldurn downcast," Herkimer told them when he caught the two off to one side and out of earshot. "I not only feel my gratitude to you two for givin' me back my gold mine, but I can show my feelings in a real practical way. I'm giving each of you a share in the Dollar Sign Gold Mine." He waved a precautionary finger. "Oh, it won't be any great chunk of fortune, boys, but five-six years from now, when the roads are built and the machinery installed and the mine in full operation you'll find you got a real nice little piece of income to fall back on if things get tough."

The hunter slapped Herkimer solidly on the back. "Herk, old man, I always knew you were the salt of the earth—whatever that is." He bent closer to the old man's ear. "And just for the hell of it, old boy, just where the hell *did* you hide those gold pokes?"

Herkimer scratched his head, scratched his belly, scratched his crotch.

"Now, why didn't you ask me that five minutes ago? I'd have told you right off. Now it's clean slipped my mind again."

"I thought it might have," the hunter said. "Next time that happens, old-timer, I suggest you look at your boot heels and shirtsleeves. That dried red clay is a dead giveaway."

He left Herkimer with his mouth hanging open and went over to pump Fairfeather's limp hand.

"Don't look so despondent, friend. After all, virtue is its own reward."

"Oh, go to hell! You didn't come off a damn bit better than I did, smart guy."

"I know, so there's nothing to do but mop up my tears and find some other deal to replace my broken dreams. *Adios, amigo.*"

He went to his horse, swung into the saddle and turned

its head back in the direction of the Spondulix Mine. At the head of the tunnel he climbed down and went inside. The freight wagon stood just around a bend in the stope, Butch Quant's box of gold dust sitting solidly in the middle of the wagon bed. The team was hitched just beyond, munching contentedly on a rack of hay.

Whistling, he hitched the team and drove out into the burning daylight. He was tying his saddle horse to the tail-gate of the wagon when Herkimer said, "Like I allus maintained, you're too cute a bastard to go off and leave any loose change layin' around."

He was sitting on his horse a dozen yards away, lounging in the saddle, crossed arms leaning on the saddle horn.

"You do get around," the hunter said.

"Try to," Herkimer said. He climbed down, chuckling. "Anything I can do for you, son, just say the word."

"You can do one thing, old-timer. You were always saying you knew who carved the dollar sign on the cliff and how it was done. Was that just some more mad hermit talk?"

Herkimer dropped his voice to a hoarse whisper. "I'll tell you the God's truth, son, most of it I done all by myself with a chipping hammer, a short sledge and a star drill. Part of it was natural cracks in the rock but I finished it off the way you saw it before it collapsed."

"Yeah?" the hunter said skeptically. "Then tell me how you got to it, under that overhang?"

Herkimer dropped his voice to a growling whisper, "I'll tell you the truth and the whole truth, son. I et eggs and et 'em and et . . . *OWOOOO!* You sonuvabitch, you got no call to kick an old man, 'specially not in a delicate place like that."